She Walks On Water

A novel

by Cecil Bothwell

Brave Ulysses Books
2013

She Walks On Water
ISBN-13: 978-1484009208
Copyright © 2013 by Cecil Bothwell
cover art/design by the author

Brave Ulysses Books
POB 1877
Asheville, North Carolina 28802
braveulysses.com

also by the author
•*Gorillas in the Myth: A Duck Soup Reader*
2000/second edition 2008
•*The Icarus Glitch: Another Duck Soup Reader*
2001
•*Finding Your Way in Asheville*
2005/2013
•*The Prince of War: Billy Graham's Crusade for
a Wholly Christian Empire*
2007
•*Garden My Heart: Organic Strategies for
Backyard Sustainability*
2008
•*Pure Bunkum: Reporting on the life and crimes
of Buncombe County Sheriff Bobby Lee Medford*
2008
•*Can we have archaic and idiot? A collection of
fictitious tropes*
2009
•*Whale Falls: An exploration of belief and its
consequences*
2010

She
Walks
On
Water

for Alex

I have seen them riding seaward on the waves
Combing the white hair of the waves blown back
When the wind blows the water white and black.

We have lingered in the chambers of the sea
...By sea-girls wreathed with seaweed red and brown
Till human voices wake us, and we drown.

-T.S. Eliot
The Love Song of J. Alfred Prufrock

Léogâne, Haiti

Mercredi, 13 January 2010

"We ... are, we ... are, we ... are, we ... are, we ... are." The clickety polytonal chorus billowed in slow cadence. Breathing in, "we." Breathing out, "are." In. Out.

"We."

"Are"

"We ... hear, we ... hear. your ... cry, we ... hear. May ... waters, waters ... open, waters ... open, breathe ... girl, breathe ... breathe, moon ... silver, blue ... water, things ... go, better with ... Coke, we ... swim, we ... sing, we ... sing, your ... cry."

Mellisonant voices flowed on. "We ... breathe, your ... breath, we ... sing, your ... cry, we ... hear, your ... echo, blue ... waters, waters ... open, waters ... open. We are, we are, we are. Sweet ... dreams, are ... made, of ...these."

A dark figure stirs. Moves a finger. Moves a leg. Raises an arm. Smooth skin meets rough concrete. The young woman murmurs, grimacing in pain and confusion, "You are? What are you? Where am I?"

"We are, we are, we are. Singing ... waves, sing ... ing, we ... are, Silver ... singer, I ... am, you deserve ... a break today, moon silver, moon golden, we swim, sing girl, sing girl, your name."

The battered girl gropes toward understanding. She feels more than sees cascading images of dolphins coursing through the waves. She's among them, rising to breathe and sliding through the water. "Annejoule," she says. Rather, thinks. "Annejoule I am."

Other sweet voices emerge in a chorus, "Anne ... joule, Anne ... joule, Anne ... joule. Sing ... ing, your ... name, we ... are, singing fish, singing stars, moon calling, calling moon. I'll get... him hot, show him ... what I've got, Annejoule, Annejoule. Moon silver, moon golden, we swim, swim on."

Annejoule shifts. A metallic ache courses through the back of her head. She opens her eyes to a grey concrete slab less than a meter from her face. Her head hurts so. Her leg. She blinks. What hit her? A baby wails in the distance. Every part of her body burns with pain. Abruptly, she remembers the earthquake.

Eyes wide now, shot through with terror, she feels the ground dancing beneath her bare feet, hearing the screams of neighbors, barking dogs, grating of wood against stone against brick against concrete, a deep bass rumbling and the cold shock of realization that the building, her home, her world, everything was collapsing around her. Suddenly an aftershock wells up from deep beneath the earth. Every gut feeling inside coalesces in pure terror, she screams again as she had the day before, and screams again, then relapses once more into unconsciousness.

The voices return, "Anne ... joule, Anne ... joule, Anne ... joule." Though the cadence remains the same, keeping time with her breath, in, out, in, out, her understanding seems to swell, filling in words between words, ideas between ideas. "Singing the moon we are, singing squid, squidididdly, squididance, squidapple, squideemish, I want your love, and I want your revenge, I want your love, I don't wanna be friends, numberless stars, the moon is calling, calling the golden moon. Annejoule, Annejoule. The moon is dark, the moon is light and we swim on, singing your name, I'm lovin' it, we sing. We are, we are, we are."

One voice emerges from the rest, "Silver Singer I am, Annejoule, Silver Singer. From first breath we have waited, breathed and waited, breathed and waited. You are the first Annejoule, you are the first of the Noisemakers. You hear us, you hear us, we hear you, we hear you. Singing the silver moon we sing. Noisemaker Annejoule we sing for your hearing. We sing for your song."

"Who are you," the girl thinks, or says, or thinks she says. Did she say it aloud? The voices are inside her head. "Where am I? Who are you? Who are you Silver Singer?"

"We are, we are, we are," comes the chorus. "We sing, we swim, the silver sea."

Kushimoto, Japan

Mokuyōbi, 14 January, 2010

Matsumoto Naoki rubbed his eyes with both fists and exhaled, then stretched, rolled his chair back from the desk, stood and stretched again. "As an instrument of torture this organic chemistry would suit," he muttered, gazing at the flat screen above his keypad. "Pah! For one night, enough," then scrolled the cursor to shut down the machine and crossed the small room to the oshiire closet and pulled his shikibuton from the top shelf.

After unrolling the mattress and tossing the bean-filled makura to the head, Naokimat turned off the ceiling light, opened the sliding glass door and stepped out onto the narrow balcony.

Seven stories below, traffic had thinned from its cacophonous daytime crush, but the sidewalks were still busy and commercial lights blinked and flashed. He looked up and out across the rooftops toward the harbor. To the right, the glow of tiny headlights revealed traffic on the arched Kii Oshima bridges and beyond the bridges a few bright points on the horizon announced ships coming or going. Out of sight behind the dark mass of the island sat the Oshima Experiment Station, his workplace three days each week. The lighthouse beam swung through its slow arc four times before he returned to his room, undressed and settled on the futon pad.

Sunday, he decided, would be an excellent time to ride to the harbor to visit with Chicako. And in just a few minutes the weary oceanography student drifted into sleep.

Léogâne, Haiti

Jeudi, 14 January 2010

Annejoule wakens, hearing her name weakly whispered in the near distance.

"Annejoule, mon bébé doux, Annejoule."

"Maman?" she replies, instantly recognizing the source. "Maman?"

From the dark tunnel down past her feet, a cavern formed by collapsed concrete slabs, the voice repeats.

"Annejoule, bébé, o mon bébé, Annejoule."

By sitting halfway, bending double and then crawling into the darkness, the girl creeps toward the whispering voice.

"Maman, Maman, Je suis ici."

"Mon bébé doux. Je taime."

Hands meet and grasp. The larger hand convulses, grips hard, and fails.

"Maman. Maman?" The smaller hand shakes the larger, now limp.

Annejoule crawls closer, turning her head sideways to move beneath the slab and kiss her mother's unconscious face, feeling the shallow breath on her own.

"Maman?" Louder. "Maman?" Crying. "Maman?" Screaming. "Maman?"

She gropes further into the darkness where her mother's thighs are crushed and trapped, concrete slab above, concrete floor below. The floor is stickily wet.

Though she can barely wrap her arms around her
mother's head, jammed between the floor and former ceiling,
Annejoule makes a desperate attempt, scraping skin against the
coarse cement, sobbing, urging life into the dying woman with
every fiber of her being.

"Maman ..."

Help. She needed help. Annejoule crawled backward over
chunks of crumbled concrete and finally emerged into a jangled
twilight tableau. In the failing light she gazed at a silent broken
world. Remnants of buildings that had delimited her
neighborhood were in a dozen states of collapse. She couldn't see
any movement, and cast a tentative shout into the shadows.

"Aide moi!"

Her voice seemed barely to penetrate the gloom. Louder
then, "Aide! Veuillez !" and next a scream, "Aide!" that echoed
amidst the ruins.

Nothing stirred, but again the now muffled sound of a
baby crying.

Completely drained, and sobbing now herself, Annejoule
crawled back beneath the ruins and cradled her mother's head in
her arms. An inescapable smell of blood and urine and dust and
fruit and sweat and vomit and flowers closed in.

The bereft girl breathed it in. Breathed it out. And
followed her grief and shock into sleep. Sometime during the
night her mother stopped breathing.

Kushimoto, Japan

Kinyōbi, 15 January, 2010

Naokimat rolled into his parking slot, clicked a cable lock around the frame and front wheel of his bicycle, then slung his book bag over his shoulder as he strode toward the research station buildings. This morning's discussion would involve the basics of stereochemistry, and despite the long night of study, he felt sure he hadn't gleaned enough, scrolling through the complex powerpoint downloaded from the professor's Web page. The inflexible research director embraced an assumption that all students would arrive fully familiar with the weekly lesson. His mockery of the uninformed was embarrassing in the extreme.

Naoki's cell phone hummed, Chicako's face appeared on the screen and he answered in text.

CLPNG 1 HND

JBO SHRMP A pause. SNDY C-U?

!! 8 AM. NOW CLSS

CLPNG 1 HND

"Naokisan!" The shout was from another research fellow.

"Takusan!" he responded. `'Three dimensional bonding. Understanding proved easy?"

"Gave up. Until late 98Koshien I played and ..."

"Video baseball? Today's discussion approaching?"

His friend grinned, "Baseball I understand."

The conversation continued as they climbed the stairs to the university building and into its cool corridor.

Léogâne, Haiti

Vendredi, 15 January 2010

"Anne-joule, Anne-joule, we sing your name. You are the first, the first of the Noisemakers. Don't ya wanta be a Fanta? From first breath and through all the breathing we have waited Anne-joule." Again a single voice came to the fore. "Annejoule, I feel your sorrow."

Stirring in her sleep, the girl answers. "Who are you, where are you? Where am I? Who are you Silver Singer?"

"We are, we are, we are," chorused the voices. "You are, as Wave Whisperer, an orphan, Anne-joule. We sing your sorrow. We sing your breath. We sing your mother. We sing your heart."

An orphan. Annejoule wakens abruptly, with a gasp. She touches her mother's cold face, kisses her once again, and pulls away. An orphan. Hunger clawed at her gut, and thirst. Backing from the narrow concrete lean-to she emerges into morning light, blinking at the brightness and trying to take in the scope of the altered landscape. Nothing is as it should be.

One room in the shattered building before her had been home and floral workshop for the three of them. Her mother, her brother and ... her brother. Where was Justinien?

"Justy!" Her voice sounded strange. Strangled. "Justy!"

The upper floors of the apartment block were sandwiched and canted, five levels no taller now than two in some places. Living in the lowest level, a basement almost, and set against the hillside, had spared Annejoule's life, the embankment preventing a complete collapse of the floor above.

She gazed up the pile, saw a detached arm caught on a wire, and two feet jutting out beneath the fourth floor deck. An infant, probably Marianne's bebe, Laban, was wailing, unseen, somewhere overhead.

"Justy!" She cried out again, and began to slowly circle the pile that had been home.

Annejoule glanced around to see that the entire neighborhood had come down. Her whole world compressed. A sandwich beneath a rock. A cockroach beneath a heel. Here and there a bit of a building remained recognizable. The few trees offered living signposts. Signposts with their destinations obliterated.

She struggled to grasp the enormity of change. Nothing was as it had been. Everything new, but ruined, ruined beyond the ruination that had always and ever been normal life in urban Haiti. Rags shredded into smaller rags. Dust ground to finer dust. Sadness flatter than sadness.

At the next building over, two men were digging into the rubble with their bare hands, flinging broken cement and shreds of wood behind them, uncaring where it fell. Slumped against a tree, Penouel stared blankly, tears streaming down his dusted face. He was muttering, inaudibly, names, names, names. The sound of women wailing, men sobbing, children shrieking, began to register as Annejoule attempted to come to terms with the shift.

"Justy!" she called again, circling the ruin.

There was no reply.

Skyward, Laban resumed his cries and Annejoule found herself climbing stairs, cognizant that someone had to tend to the infant and discovering that the stairwell was the only completely intact section of the collapsed apartment block. At the fourth floor she gazed through a door opening at a hallway which fell away at a fairly steep angle. Some walls remained intact and others lay in varying states of ruin. The baby crawled out of a doorway thirty meters down slope, bawling.

"Laban!" she called, and he turned his head, wide eyed.

Annejoule looked down at the half meter gap between the doorway and the hallway floor, swallowed hard and jumped. Was it her imagination, or did the floor slab move as she landed? She stood stock still while her heartbeat slowed, then she started forward, stepping lightly down the sharply canted hall and keenly atuned to any motion in the buildng.

Laban was crawling toward her now and as the distance closed she suddenly noticed another gap in the concrete between them, this one more than a meter wide. The youngster was quickly approaching the chasm. Annejoule broke into a run, reached the gaping fracture and without breaking stride leapt across. She laughed aloud in relief at her safe landing and quickly caught the two-year-old in her arms.

"Laban! Bebe! You're safe now," and she hugged him to her chest, patting his back as his crying subsided.

She moved down the sloping hall to the doorway that opened into what had been Marianne's apartment. A jagged edge of the floor slab ended abruptly just centimeters from the door. Annejoule eased toward the edge and peered over to see the jumble of furniture, clothing, kitchen wares, concrete, wood and glass below. A human figure was visible, largely obscured by rubble, the top third crushed under a section of an upper floor. Through the dust she recognized Marianne's dress. Nausea welled up, and she turned back to the hallway.

The gap she had easily leapt running downhill looked daunting now. Could she run and jump uphill, carrying a child? Peering down she considered the possibility of clambering deeper into the collapsed building, to find some other route. The prospect of broken bodies and the uncertainty of the attempt put her off. To her right, a door hung all but torn from its hinges.

Annejoule propped Laban against the wall. "Stay, bebe. Stay there. Okay?"

The boy wimpered but sat still.

She grabbed the wooden door by both knobs and pulled, and again, harder this time, and she nearly fell backward as it broke free. Then she dragged the thing, lighter than she'd expected, but flimsier than she'd hoped, and flopped it across the gap at its narrowest point. It would have to do.

Then she scooped up Laban and sprang across her bridge, which slid backward as she pushed off her second step and fell, clattering into the gap. Annejoule continued uphill toward the stairwell where she stepped hastily across the upper break.

Suddenly the building began to move as another aftershock jolted the landscape. The hallway Annejoule had just exited crumbled downward another meter or more, as she clutched the baby to herself and cried out.

The stairwell held.

Léogâne, Haiti

Samadi, 16 January 2010

"We are, we are, we are." Annejoule now heard the litany both waking and sleeping, though it faded to the background when she was focussed on a task at hand. Sometimes just Silver Singer, but more often a chorus. "We sing, we sing, we sing the silver sea." And between the words, squeaks and groans, sometimes birdlike, sometimes bellows.

After rescuing Laban, she had turned her attention to the necessities of food and water. A rain barrel, half broken in the quake still held several liters, and she and the baby had soon slaked their thirst. She remembered a basket of akee fruit she had picked with her mother, and guessed that the angled slab might have spared it in the back corner of their room. Only the intensity of her hunger and the need to feed Laban steeled her to the prospect of crawling past her mother's body, which she immediately discovered had already acquired a faint stench of death.

"Maman, Maman," she whispered as she pushed past the corpse, "I love you Maman." Back and back into the darkness she inched her way, trying to identify the objects in her path. A tin cup, clumps of clothing, broken dishes, a broom, her mother's prized knife. A small, swollen foot.

She had exhaled hard, too overcome to scream. "Justy," she cried, "Oh, Justy." The tears she had suppressed of necessity, and the overpowering sense of loss, welled up and burst through.

"Oh Justinien, Maman, what am I to do?" It took many long minutes to collect herself, with the only small comfort the singing of the voices in her mind. "We are, we are, we are. Annejoule we sing your name."

A little further on Annejoule's hand closed on the fruit basket, and feeling around she discovered a partial loaf of bread. Backing out she collected the cup and knife and, moving more quickly than she'd entered, soon emerged into sunlight again and hurried to the rain barrel where she dipped out a full cupful and swished her mouth and spat, attempting to shed the rank odor of the dead.

Several of the akee had ripened and yawned before the quake. With her mother's knife, she cut away the fleshy arils, then tossed away the seeds and rind. It would be better cooked, but raw would do. Laban ate a little, mashing it between his fingers before tasting and swallowing. Then she cut them each a bit of the dry bread and completed their meager meal.

"Maman?" he'd asked, looking up at Annejoule.

"Orphans," she replied. "Both of us."

"Maman?" he'd asked again.

"Maman," she sighed. "Maman."

They had slept, and now ate, under a rough lean-to Annejoule had fashioned from broken boards and two pieces of metal roofing, the protection necessitated more by sun than any chance of rain in the island's driest season. Sun and an urgent need for some feeling of shelter from the events of the past few days.

She hadn't spoken to anyone other than Laban, though

other people were moving about the neighborhood, some digging, some carrying their belongings, many weeping. Apart from the two of them, there seemed to be no survivors from her apartment building, and no one digging into the rubble.

By Saturday afternoon foot traffic on the road had picked up and two men with wheelbarrows had passed several times, up the street with a pair of folded corpses and down again, empty. Up with two more bodies, down again.

"We must bury Maman and Justinien," she whispered to Laban, "But how can we get them from the building?"

Kushimoto, Japan

Nichiyōbi, 17 January, 2010

Traffic was light as Naokimat maneuvered downhill toward the harbor, past the junior high school, then onto the peninsula road. It was warmer than normal for mid-January and the onshore breeze carried traces of bunker oil and dead fish from the industrial docks to his left. A few figures moved along the wharf and a knot of gulls swarmed above a fishing vessel where seamen were offloading their catch.

He veered left onto the harbor road and then right, braking as he approached the low building that was both home and workshop to the shipwright Yamamoto. He leaned the bike against a sturdy bamboo fence and followed a short garden path to the door which was answered by the smiling, bowing patriarch.

Naoki returned the gesture, saying,"Ojisan, the day fair is."

"Musuko Matsumoto, welcome." The elder's eyes showed amusement as he asked, "On Sunday few the repairs we do. You in particular need are?"

Accustomed to the old man's jibes, Naoki was yet a little tongue-tied and stammered, "Fair day I think the coast road to ride."

"And company desired ..." Yamamoto replied, his face wreathed by his grin. He turned into the house and called gently, "Chicayam, at the door, a strange young man is waiting."

Momentarily Chicako appeared beside her grandfather,

black hair pulled back into a pony tail, wearing a brilliant red blouse atop pants that matched her hair, and carrying a small daypack. "Naokisan, good it is you to see." Then to her elder, "Oji Yam, my good friend you did not suggest to enter ?"

With clear enjoyment the old man replied, "Matsumoto me to visit did not come. Uncomfortable dancing foot-to-foot would the case be, I think. Now you two, off. Enjoy. Fair the day is." He bowed and disappeared into the hall.

Chicako shook her head, "Forgive ..."

But her boyfriend interrupted. "Forgiveness is, and gentle torment your Oji Yamamoto enjoys. To visit him I did not ride."

Soon they were chatting excitedly, both on bicycles and headed down the Kii peninsula road. Passing the Oshima bridge they left the commercial port behind and began to catch intermittent views of low surf breaking on the bouldered shore.

"Where to?" Chicako queried. "Shiono Misaki Ojisan I told."

"Than the Shiono lighthouse quieter places exist."

"And you prefer ...?"

"Quieter places," he replied, flashing her a quick grin.

After passing through Itsumo with its small port, and then through a short tunnel, Naoki crossed the road, dismounted and started down a dirt trail with Chicako close behind.

"This is?" she queried.

"Quieter," he replied. "Out to the point this trail leads. Here you've not been?"

Soon they locked their bikes to a tree and continued along a trail that overlooked a rugged coast. Twenty minutes later the trail descended to a sheltered cove with a short stretch of coarse sand and low surf reduced to subdued lapping by natural jetties on either hand. The only sound was a distant crushing of waves and a few seabirds.

Naoki kicked off his shoes and quickly stripped to his swimsuit before trotting down the strand and tumbling into the sea, the surging water just a little warmer than the dry winter air.

Moments later, Chicako followed. Shoulder deep, they embraced and kissed, the warmth between them charged by the ocean's relative heat.

"Lunch you packed?" Naoki asked.

"Food your thought while holding me?" Chicako put both hands on his head and pushed him under. When he came up spluttering she added, "Bentos, and apples."

"One hand clapping," was his reply as he pulled her into another embrace.

Léogâne, Haiti

Dimanche, 17 January 2010

"Annejoule you are the first of the Noisemakers, the first Annejoule! We sing, we sing."

"Why do you call me Noisemaker?" she replied.

"You, your kind, you do not much sing. You ride the sea in hard-skinned upturned islands. Be all that you can be. Above the waves. Below the waves. Noise. Noise. Noise. Always noise."

"And why am I the first?"

"Annejoule, Annejoule, we sing your name. You are the first to hear us, the first to answer, the first since first breath. Billie Jean is not my lover. You are. You are. You are."

"Where are you?"

"The bay. The bay. The bay."

The baby stirred and fretted, tucked in close beside her, and Annejoule opened her eyes. The sun was already bright, the metal roof warming, and it suddenly struck her that it must be late on Sunday morning and there were no church bells.

"No noisemaking today," she whispered.

In the first days after—and that's how the world seemed to her now, the world after, the apartment after, her life after, after Maman, after Justinien—she had been too stunned, too shocked, too terribly sad, to do much at all, but the fact of "after" had proved exhausting, and last night she had finally collapsed and slept long hours. Today she would collect herself, somehow. Move on.

Food. She must find more food. There was little else in the family apartment, she knew, nor would she go back into what was now her familial crypt. But the contents of five floors, some sixty units, lay sandwiched in chaos, and there was bound to be something edible amidst the wreckage. Laban was still asleep, so she slid away and rose without waking him and went out to begin her search.

The floors were less tightly collapsed near the stairwell, and she could stand in part of the first ground level unit. Gadite's unit. Annejoule was relieved to see no sign of Gadite or her children, though the death smell had begun to fill the air suggesting bodies all around without specificity. She found a tin of rice, a bag of beans and a few small dried fish, and set them on the stairs.

Across the hall, where Dacien and Tahirra had lived, she had to crawl to gain entry, but the overwhelming stench drove her back, out into the fresh air. Out to continue the search.

Up one floor, where Caissie and Tomas had lived above Gadite, she had to crouch immediately, but made it to a table where she found a partial loaf of bread, a sweet potato and a mango.

Mangoes! Of course. She could pick all she wanted just a short way out of town over toward the bay. She hurried back down the steps, collected her earlier finds and went back to the lean-to, where Laban was awake and complaining. Soon enough she had cut up the fruit and some bread by way of breakfast, and the child seemed happier.

"Happier than I will ever be again," she thought.

Kushimoto, Japan

Suiyōbi , 20 January, 2010

Naokimat yawned and leaned back in his chair, wearied as usual by the philosophy lecturer. His making much of thrice-split hairs. Belaboring the obvious garnered small interest. At least with online lectures the teachers were unable to see their students' bored reactions.

His thoughts turned back to the previous day's conversation with Takusan. His friend had related a story beyond belief, that fishermen in Taiji were slaughtering dolphins on an immense scale, to market the meat, and with government approval.

"Many thousands, Naokisan, thousands! Some North Americans in secret filmed, and there the story is being told."

That such butchery could be happening, without wide public knowledge, seemed impossible. And who would knowingly eat dolphin? It was nowhere to be seen in food stores or stalls. Was it being sold to the Chinese? The Koreans? Takusan must be wrong, but where would information be available to counter his tale?

Surely one or another of the professors in the oceanography program would know of this, would have said something to the students, would have spoken out. Oceanic ecology was so much at threat, no senseless slaughter of keystone species could be left unchallenged.

Takusan forwarded links to English language Web sites

that claimed to document the carnage, but his limited interpretive skills and the mixed-up translation on Babelfish left him deeply uncertain. He read:

Be slaughtered more than 20000 dolphins in Japan may from September each year. Fishermen using hundreds of sound barriers and bewildered, like regular migration from introduction in desperate pod hidden lagoon in Roundup

He'd definitely need to ask a professor. It just didn't seem possible that such butchery was going on without general public awareness.

Still and all, his nation's history showed that strange, even unbelievably grotesque secrets were often successfully kept. Minimata's mercury poisoning had gone on for years, damaging a generation, before the problem was acknowledged.

Ca Ira, Haiti

Lundi, 25 January 2010

During the preceding week, Annejoule had made her way down the dirt roads running south from town, where she remembered seeing numberless mangoes in past years. But she quickly discovered that fruit in easy reach from the ground had been picked clean, and many taller trees had been hacked down. After long hours of searching she had only found three ripe fruits which she carefully nestled in the burlap shoulder bag she'd discovered along the road. By late afternoon Laban had become more and more restless and fretful so she'd given up on her search. Along the way she wondered about her friend, Ghislaine, whether she had survived and how she might be faring.

Back in her neighborhood she begged workmen to excavate her former home, to recover her mother's and brother's bodies, but to no avail.

"There are others still living," they insisted. "Finding them comes first."

"Please ...?"

"Later. The dead won't return, and they won't leave. Gone beneath the waves they are."

The smell of death now permeated the neighborhood, breathed in with each breath, tasted on the tongue, thick and foul. On upper floors of the collapsed apartments, birds squawked and bickered over putrefying carrion that had been her neighbors. A dog ran down the street carrying a child's arm, with other dogs in hot pursuit. She shuddered. Could worse be imagined?

Annejoule mounded rubble over the angular opening into her old home to prevent animal entry, scraped and gathered dirt to fill the interstices, repurposing the place into a tomb, then topping the mound with a crudely fashioned cross as she muttered a bit of a prayer to Damballa and Bondye and the Christian god Ghislaine had learned of in her church.

By mid-week, the scant water in the rain barrel was gone and she'd found only a little food in searching other apartments, a bag of rice in one and a partial sack of flour in another. Then a box of matches. On a foray into a neighboring building on Thursday she had run into an older boy carrying two plastic jugs.

"Where did you find water?" she queried.

"What can you pay?"

"Nothing. I have nothing."

"Oh, you can pay." He looked her up and down. "You are a woman," he smirked and thrust his hips toward her. "You can pay me."

"No." All but unthinking, her hand found the handle of her Mother's knife in her shoulder bag.

He dropped the containers and grabbed her arms. "If you won't pay, I'll take what I want." Then he snatched at her skirt and ripped up, baring her leg to her hip. Annejoule whipped out the knife and swung it toward his face.

"Get away! I'll cut you! I'll hurt you!"

The boy backed away, leering and laughing. "I'll come back with friends. I know where you're camped. You'll give what I want soon enough." He snatched up his water and turned away.

Shaking, she watched him until he disappeared around a corner, then hurried toward home. Friends. He had friends and she had Laban. The neighborhood was no longer safe, and there was little food and no water.

An hour later she had tied together a few rags and some clothing, a length of rope, a small aluminum cook pot and, with her mother's knife, the matches, rice, beans, flour and one remaining dried fish in her shoulder bag, took Laban's hand and walked away from her Mother, her brother, her home. A few streets up she turned left and followed the road that led toward the coast. She knew there were farm fields and more mango trees in the few kilometers between Léogâne and the coast, but had no real destination in mind.

Collapsed buildings lined the road and everywhere people were digging. An ancient hotel had been reduced to little more than splinters and dust, but for the glass front doors, intact within their frame and bearing the instruction "Poussez." Annejoule laughed aloud, taken by the incongruity of it all. A "push" might collapse the last bit standing, but push was all she had to offer against the collapse of her world. Push on, push out, breathe in, breathe out.

"Sing, Annejoule, sing. Double your pleasure, double your fun. We breathe your name." The voices in her head continued.

The town gave way to greenery as evening settled, and a young dog began to trail her. "Got no food," she told it. The pup reacted by wagging its tail and hopping a few yards closer.

"Really. Got no food," she repeated and it dashed in front of her and sat, tail still in motion. She bent to scratch between its ears and the wagging spread from tail to head.

"Suit yourself, but you'll need a name. Poussez. Poussez you are. Poussez meet Laban, and I am Annejoule."

On they walked, three now looking for food and shelter and some kind of future. As they neared the village of Ca Ira and night closed in, Annejoule veered from the main road onto a side track between two farm fields and helped herself to overhanging mangoes. Even Poussez ate a bit as she shared the juicy prizes with Laban, and, touched by the dog's evident hunger, she dug in her bag and produced the dried fish. "Here you go, Poussez. You owe me one."

The dog eagerly accepted the gift and lay down to chew the leathery treat. Soon the threesome lay curled in soft grass, weary and thirsty, but safe for another night.

"Fish Annejoule. Fish. The bay, Annejoule. The bay. We sing your name."

Kushimoto, Japan

Suiyōbi, 27 January, 2010

"Takusan, to Taiji cycling is possible. Twenty kilometers, no more."

"The story now you believe?" Takusan grinned.

"Worthy of examination. No classes, 26 Nigatsu, coastal cycling and camping is ..."

"Is done." The two friends bumped fists, and set to planning their adventure.

Ca Ira, Haiti

Mercredi, 27 January 2010

On Tuesday the trio had followed a dirt track to a slowly moving stream, La Rouyonne. Poussez leapt into the water, slaking her thirst with great slurping laps, Laban quickly followed, and Annejoule reluctantly, recalling her Mother's warnings about water-borne disease, but too parched to long stand on caution.

The path and the muddy stream ran beside cultivated fields, and a furtive incursion garnered a double-handful of ripening beans which she shared with the toddler and the dog. Thieving troubled her, but hunger spoke more loudly than conscience and the past two weeks had been the hungriest she'd known in an often-hungry life.

They found shelter from the sun under a spreading canopy of ginger and had slept more peacefully, not so famished and feeling safe in their seclusion.

"Sing, we sing. Annejoule, we sing your name. Plop, plop, fizz, fizz."

In the morning, Annejoule had slipped into the next garden plot along the way, eyeing tomatoes that hung in profusion from a carefully staked vine. As she reached for a ripened fruit, a thin voice caught her short. Her feet felt nailed to the ground.

"Your name child?"

She turned to face a withered crone, bent and graying, but smiling all the same.

"Annejoule."

The old woman nodded. "You must be hungry Annejoule, stealing tomatoes from tired old Jeanine."

"I am half starved, Madame Jeanine. I know stealing is wrong, but since ..."

"Yes, since. Where is your family, Annejoule?"

"Fanmi mwen, Maman et Justinien, se mort."

"Justinien ... papa a ou?

"I don't know my papa. Justy was my young brother."

Poussez came bounding into the clearing, followed by Laban.

Eyebrows raised, Jeanine simply asked, "And?"

"Laban, Maria's baby, an orphan like myself. And Poussez, who joined us on the road."

"Pick some tomatoes, Annejoule, and follow me."

She gingerly pulled off a couple of sun-warm fruits, and the trio followed the old woman up a dirt lane to a tiny shack, walls a hodge-podge of bamboo and roofing panels, and the shed roof composed of similar, rusting, tin. A few chickens scratched and cooed in the shadow of a ragged bush. A sunshade of thatched bamboo and sawgrass covered the space in front of the structure, and the perimeter of the yard was lined with sea shells, coral, driftwood and miscellaneous plastic objects.

The old woman stepped inside and emerged with two bananas which she handed to her visitors, and a small crust of bread which she tossed to the dog. "Jeanine doesn't have much, but she's not hungry today and so better off than some." She sank to the ground and sat cross-legged against the front wall.

"You come from Léogâne?" When Annejoule nodded, she inquired further, "Is it bad there?"

"So many buildings down. Still digging for survivors. So many dead. Everything gone. No water. No food. Very bad." Recalling her assailant she added, "Bad people. A young thug threatened me ..."

"Usually people come together in hardship, but some will take what they can get." The elder nodded, knowingly. "Jeanine felt the earth shake, but nothing to fall down out here." She gestured upward, "And nothing to fall down on Jeanine. Nothing but the stars."

Ca Ira, Haiti

Samedi, 30 January 2010

Jeanine had only scarcity to share, yet shared it willingly, and had urged Annejoule to stay with her, "For just a while, my child. You need a home."

The girl in turn had hastened to prove her worth, adding the rice and flour to their combined stores, and presenting Jeanine with the matches as well.

"Matches are a prize, sweet girl. A prize! With a bit of charcoal or driftwood, we could now cook a feast," the elder had observed, "Though we've not much to cook. The rice we can simply soak. I've plenty of dried manioc."

On the second night in the shack Annejoule's dreams had been even more vivid, the voices louder and more insistent.

"We sing. We sing. We sing you to the bay. Annejoule, the bay Annejoule, the bay." And the song was so sweet, the voices so endearing, as not to be refused. At first light she slipped from the shack, Poussez on her heels, and followed the path by La Rouyonne toward the coast. They splashed through a small tributary stream as the stream widened into a pool, and skirted its shore.

Annejoule had been told that spirits of the dead often entered streams and wondered as she waded if her Maman and Justy swirled around her feet. "Maman?" she asked aloud. "Maman?" There was no answer from the grey-green turbulence.

But perhaps her family's spirits had sped to Guinee, the

home of the gods. Annejoule hoped they were happy, whereever death had taken them.

Soon she heard waves dashing against rocks and then, over a low dune, she saw the turquoise sea, closed her eyes and simply breathed the tart salt air. Each breath seemed to cleanse her of the taste and the remembered stench of death, of the terror and the loss.

"Breathe girl. Breathe. Silver Singer I am.

"Annejoule, Annejoule, we sing your name."

She opened her eyes and gazed across the wide gulf toward Ile de la Gonave on the horizon. Then much nearer, she spied fins cresting through the waves, headed her direction. A pod of dolphins was leaping and frisking its way toward shore, some of them spinning in mid-air before they crashed back into the waves, and the voices in her head grew clearer.

"Annejoule, Noisemaker. You are the first Annejoule. Ever we have waited. Ever we have known."

She continued down the slope, between scattered rocks and onto the bleached sand and gravel of the strand. The dolphins kept approaching, two ahead of the others right up into the shallows as she waded past her knees. Reaching her they stopped short, and each released a fresh-killed snapper that floated within easy reach, then they turned. Meanwhile the dog ran back and forth on the beach, barking in excitement.

The larger dolphin surfaced, rolled to one side, and fixed the girl with a steady gaze as the sweet voice sounded in her mind.

"Silver Singer I am. Annejoule, we sing your name."

"Thank you," she thought in a way that felt more like

speaking than thinking. "I sing yours."

She hooked a finger into the gill slit of each fish and almost danced back to Jeanine's shack, dragging a bleached branch and singing one of her Mother's songs aloud.

> *"La Siren, La Balenn,*
> *Chapo'm tonbe nan la me.*
> *La Siren, La Balenn,*
> *Chapo'm tonbe nan la me."*

Kushimoto, Japan

Suiyōbi, 10 February, 2010

The school term slogged by, Naoki by turns bored with his philosophy and statistics classes, and impatient that the molecular biology and tidal ecosystems curriculum seemed so measured. Work at the research station often came down to little more than shoveling chopped mackerel to the captive bluefins. And while the purpose of the project was urgent, providing farm raised tuna in a world where wild stocks were being fished to extinction, his role didn't amount to meaningful scientific exploration. Another year of lectures and exams blocked his escape.

Despite his frequently expressed preference for video games, Takusan seemed to be keeping up with his classwork, and the pair studied together many afternoons.

"Co-valent bonding"

"Chromatosome."

"e. coli replicates"

And on and on.

Meanwhile, he had only managed two more dates with Chicako, a short visit and a walk around the commercial piers, with her grandfather Yamamoto much more effective as a gatekeeper than he would have preferred. They texted regularly, however, and he'd filled her in on the plan he and Takusan had made for the cycling trip to Taiji.

"+ U?" he'd queried.

";^)" she'd answered. "BUT OJI YAM"

"MST B PSSBLE WNTNG U "

"ME 2 U"

"XXNG FNGRS"

"JBO SHRMP"

"CLPNG 1 HND"

Ca Ira, Haiti

Dimanche, 14 February 2010

The fish had pleased Jeanine no end, as had the driftwood. "My Louis was such a fisherman. But eight years he's gone ..." she paused and shook her head. "Eight years. Jeanine hasn't seen so fine a fish in all that time. How did you catch them, my sweet one?"

"The ..." she hesitated, "... maybe frightened by dolphins," Annejoule added, "Or sharks."

"Our good luck that is, thank Agwe," replied the old woman, silently noting the telltale puncture wounds left by dolphin teeth.

The four had eaten well that evening as the fish were a couple of kilos apiece. Afterward Annejoule and Laban settled back against the shack and Jeanine sat in her only chair as stars began to appear overhead.

"Louis spent his life on the ocean, He told me many tales." The woman's voice was soft and soothing and slow, conveying a sense of warm remembrance tinged with heartfelt loss. "We said goodbye so many times, and there was such joy on his return.

"Often Mambo brought storms when *mon pêcheur* was out to sea, but once ... once Louis was blown much further from home and I was sure he was lost. Always he returned at night, you see, the fishing places were so near. And that night he did not return, and the next. I wept, knowing we had said goodbye for the last time, that Agwe had pulled him below the waves, that Baron

Samedi had seized his soul. I cried tears enough to make a river.

"But the gods smiled on Jeanine, and on the third day *mon marin audacieux* came home to me. Such joy. I thanked Agwe and Mambo and Samedi and Ayida-Weddo, the ancestors and the ocean and the mountains and the moon.

"Louis told me of the waves and the wind. Waves such as he had never seen! The wind from all directions! Far, far his little boat was blown and then the biggest wave of all tossed him like a leaf and his safety rope snapped," she clapped her hands once. "Snapped! And he was thrown into the angry sea!"

"How was he saved?" gasped Annejoule. "Was it *la siren*? They say she returns her captives after three days!"

"*Non, non. C'était les dauphins de fileur,* the dolphins that spin," Jeanine replied. "Two dolphins, side-by-each, found my Louis where he swam as Mambo took the storm on its way. Where he thought he would be swallowed by the waves, two dolphins swam side-by-each and he held their fins, and they carried him back to his boat. As if they knew which was his and where he belonged. When he had bailed the water and hoisted his sail, they led him home." She sighed and shook her head. "They led *mon pêcheur* home to Jeanine."

"Did your Louis ever hear the dolphins sing?" Annjoule whispered.

"Ah, *la chanson des dauphins*," replied Jeanine, "Louis told me he heard their song, and ever he wished he understood what they were singing."

Kushimoto, Japan

Nichiyōbi, 21 February, 2010

"Sensuous tall woman my dreams through every night glides. Arousal welcome." Naokisan smiled at Chicako as they ambled toward what they now thought of as "their" cove.

"How tall?" came the reply.

Naoki raised his arm straight up, hand flat to indicate height, grinning, then lowered it gently atop his companion's dark hair. "This precisely. But different appearing," he stopped and looked her up and down. He nodded, "Appearance different."

"Another woman your dream inhabits? Well!" Chicako put her hands to her hips, her expression a mixture of amusement and insult and hurt.

"Face same," laughed Naoki, using both hands to frame his view, up and then scanning slowly down to her feet. "Hands same. Legs same. Feet same. Clothes fewer. Missing, in fact. None whatsoever."

She sprang toward him and delivered a playful slap. "Without permission," was her scolding reply.

"Dreams uncontrolled." He folded his hands and bowed. "Blameless I remain."

Chicako laughed and kissed him. "Well, I suppose ..."

"Yet were control offered," he continued, grinning, "These dreams I would not change."

They soon scrambled over the rocks and onto the sheltered beach. Naokisan set about spreading a blanket in a notch at the base of the cliff. When he looked up again, Chicako had shed her clothes.

"Like this?" she queried.

He framed her with his hands again, gazing up and down. "Beautiful," he paused. "Tall ... girl, yes."

She turned and ran into the water, where he quickly joined her.

They swam and talked, laughing and teasing. Then Naoki raised the question most on his mind. "Taiji venture you are joining?"

"Mother said always, 'Don't make waves on the quiet surface of a pond.' And Oji Yam ... " she began.

"Solution must there be ..."

Chicako continued, "Oji Yam I have told, attending Kushimoto girlfriend's house sleep-over. Kaeda the story will affirm."

"Happy I am ..."

"Unhappy, I am, Oji Yam to tell lies. Disrespect. And waves likely. But joyous with you to go." She pulled him into an embrace and they kissed briefly before a wet whistled whoosh drew their attention out to sea in time to see a dolphin blow, and then cough twice before submerging. Others soon surfaced, including some young, and they watched in silent fascination until the pod moved on out of the cove.

"Taiji visit perhaps not ... ?" the girl suggested.

"Different there. Stories of slaughter ... "

"So beautiful, and intelligent."

"Yes," Naoki pulled her into another embrace. "Like tall

woman in dreams."

Chickako whispered in his ear as she ran her hand from his shoulder down across his chest. "Surface smooth and not revealing, soft and yielding, " She pressed her fingers into his stomach, "And below," her hand moved lower, "The heat."

Later, at a climactic moment in their lovemaking, Naoki half-shouted, "Heisenberg!" Chicako, laughing, rose beneath him.

Afterward, draped across each other, limbs tangled in languor, she whispered, "Why Heisenberg?"

"When with you love I make," he answered, "If focused on where I am, determination of momentum impossible becomes."

"And vice-versa?" she asked.

He nodded.

Tenderly stroking his face Chicako replied, "Of neither ever at such times confused am I."

Ca Ira, Haiti

Dimanche, 21 February 2010

Rain had started during the night and built into torrents, hammering the hut's tin roof into metalic thunder. Laban was frightened and crying. The yard visible from the doorway had become a sea of mud and La Rouyenne, which ran a not inconsiderable distance from the shack, had swelled and overwhelmed its banks.

"Will we be swept away?" Annejoule inquired, a tinge of fear in her voice.

"Mambo willing, no," was the reply. "Louis built here on a knoll, and in fifty years the water has never reached us or damaged the garden. But for everything a time."

Annejoule looked more closely at the building's surrounds and saw that Jeanine was right. Though the rise was subtle, they were definitely situated on higher ground. She relaxed, a little at least, and gazed at the torrent. On the surface of the rushing orange and brown river all manner of garbage and flotsam rolled by, boards and clothing and plastic bottles. A dead goat bobbed and rolled, legs akimbo. Were the souls of her dear Maman and little brother swimming in that clamoring flow?

In the previous week, Annejoule had been called again to the sea, and again the dolphins had delivered fish. Jeanine had once more noticed tooth marks and this time pressed further about the girl's fishing success.

"How did you ..."

"Driven to shore by ..." pause, "spinner dolphins."

"And bitten?"

"Bitten."

"And delivered?"

Annejoule bit her lower lip and nodded.

"You witchy witchy *les dauphins*?" asked Jeanine.

"No, *grand-maman*. No. I hear them sing. 'Annejoule, Annejoule, come to the sea!' And so I go."

"This is big magic, my sweet. Big magic. Agwe has touched you."

The words were clearer each night, the dolphin songs chaining together into longer messages, and yet so strange, talking of mysteries that threaded the waves and rolled in the tide. A melange of voices, of nonsense and sense, full of joy, full of laughter, filled with squeaks and groans and whispers, and overwhelmingly, a deep sense of love. They seemed to love each other and love the ocean and love to eat and love Annejoule.

Noisy one Annejoule, we sing your song
Annejoule, Annejoule your song we sing.
We sing, we sing, we sing the day, the day.
Squidapple, squididance, squididly, the balenn.
I kissed a girl and I liked it
The taste of her cherry Chapstick
Deep, deep, oh deep. Noise and noise.
Far and far, love and love, light and dark,
The day began, the day goes on, the day goes ever on,
Jellyfish, bellyfish, round and round
Sunshine, moonshine.

What is, is. What is, is.
What's not, not. What's not, not.
Double your pleasure, double your fun,
Breathe in. Breathe out.
Now is now is now is now.
Shimmer and shimmer, spin and spin.
Song of my singing, song of my mother,
Song of begining, song of begetting,
True to be true to be true to be true,
We sing, we sing, we sing the day.
Wisdom is, wisdom does, wisdom comes,
Fish, fish, fish, fish, fish, fish.
Ocean ours, ocean ours, noisemaker noise.
Love and love and love and love.
I wish I were an Oscar Meier weiner
That is what I'd truly like to be,
We sing, we sing, we sing the day, the day.
The waters are changing Annejoule.
We do not understand.
Tell us oh tell us Annejoule.
We do not understand.

Koza, Japan

Kin'yōbi, 26 February, 2010

In the predawn, the three friends had met in the junior high school parking area, each with a day-pack and a tightly rolled shikibuton. In addition, Naokimat had strapped a tent to the rack on his bike frame, "Needless, one hopes ..." he said, looking at the starry sky, "but ..."

"Best prepared," Chicako finished.

"Weather no issue," added Takusan. "Guards and dogs, however ..."

Startled, Chicako inquired, "Guards?"

"Knowing is ..." began Naokimat.

"Knowledge of dolphin slaughter unwanted. Guards likely," intoned the other young man. "Knowledge power is."

"But danger?"

"Could be," Takusan nodded. "Could be."

"If you do not the tiger's cave enter, its cub you will not catch," added Naoki.

Once riding, however, such dark thoughts were left behind. The dawn emerged lovely, a deep rose glow on their rightward shoulders. The air was cool and dry, the road mostly untraveled at the early hour as they started north and east.

The road ran close to the coast, in some sections the salt spray touched them. Waves slammed up and over the boulders laid in as a shield from the encroaching sea. Though single-file riding made conversation all but impossible, the trio were laughing, tossing phrases back and forth, smiling with the exhilaration of the morning, the freedom and the adventure ahead. Naoki was showing-off, standing on his seat on a gentle downhill run.

Suddenly the ground shifted, no more than a hiccup really. A jerk and a jump. But it caught the clowning rider unawares and he was thrown to the roadside where he struck his head on a metal rail.

Naoki's helmet almost certainly saved his life.

Ca Ira, Haiti

Samedi, 27 February 2010

"Would you tend to Laban for a day?" Annejoule queried hopefully.

"Jeanine would be pleased, my sweet one. But what are you up to?"

"My friend, Ghislaine in Léogâne, I worry ..."

"There are bad people, and there will be much trouble. You told me yourself that the whole city fell down ... the boy who threatened ..."

"Only in daylight. I'll start back before ... and I have Poussez."

"Laban will be safe with me. Be very careful, Annejoule. And if you find matches ..." her voice trailed off, as if she were aware of asking too much.

The girl moved swiftly up the path along the brook, Poussez close on her heels. She felt excited and frightened and eager. Six weeks had passed since the quake and in her imagination much had already been set right, the city surely returned to some sort of normalcy despite the destruction of so many buildings. Perhaps she'd be able to move in with Ghislaine's family, if their apartment had survived. She wouldn't be afraid of the city with those familiar hearts close at hand.

Halfway to town, where the dirt track joined the road, she smelled sewage and death, a stench that grew stronger with each passing meter. Next she was startled to come upon hundreds of tarps and tents and many more sheets of thin plastic strung from poles and tied in a spiderweb maze of rope and string. Beneath and around the encampment, which stretched out on both sides of the thoroughfare, was a sea of mud. Grimy children stared out at her, children smeared with mud and sitting in mud, and followed her movement with baleful gazes muddied by the incomprehensibility of circumstance and surely affected by the overwhelming smell of human waste and decay. Adults with eyes barely less occluded paid her scant attention, glancing up and then back to whatever tasks they had set themselves to deal with the endless mud and the heat and the hunger.

Annejoule stopped and surveyed the blue and white expanse, understanding at once that nothing had been set right, and that everything had changed, for everyone. No matter the miracle of restoration she had grasped for in her imagination, the reality lay naked and prostrate before her. The city of her childhood had been erased. Still she moved on.

Entering the town-proper she noted hungry-eyed gleaners picking through the ruins on either hand, bricks piled, brick piles being torn apart, a very young girl crying, an older one patting her arm, starved dogs tucked into bits of shade, a child playing with an emptying oil can and dabbing at the glistening black puddle, three men arguing, two women carrying babies, an old woman conferring with a man in uniform. She quickly made her way to her former home and saw that the mounded rubble and crude cross stood undisturbed. She knelt, choking out a jumbled prayer, murmured "Maman," and "Justy" and then continued on her way, in tears.

As she walked past a tumble-down church she stepped carefully around a brightly chalked VeVe, a voudoo drawing representing Luo spirits, crossed herself and whispered "Mache chèche pa janm dòmi san soupe." She fervently hoped she deserved good fortune. Then up four blocks and over a few more Annejoule came to her friend's apartment block, appearing far more intact than her own erstwhile home. She went to Ghislaine's door and knocked, paused, knocked again, and then turned the knob, pushed and peered in.

The room was empty, and walking through it into the second she discovered it had been stripped bare. No food, utensils, tools, bedding or clothing had been left behind, though she did discover two decks of cardboard matches beside a crumpled cigarette wrapper. She tucked the matches in her sack.

For whatever cause, given the lack of despoliation, her friend and friend's family were gone without a trace. She wondered briefly if she could simply move in pending their return.

Back outside she spied a somewhat familiar face, a neighbor woman she had noticed from time to time on visits to the neighborhood.

"Ghislaine ...?" she asked

"The road to Chatulet, in a camp, or so I heard."

"How far? Do you know?"

"Two kilometers, no more. Michel said they *were* there a month past. I surely don't know today."

Koza, Japan

Doyōbi, 27 February 2010

"Singing is. Singing is. Singing is."

"Naoki I am. And you?"

Naokisan stirred, confused at the voices and experiencing the worst headache of his life. Where was he?

"We ... hear, we ... hear, your ... cry, we ... hear. May ... waters, waters ... open, waters ... open, breathe ... boy, breathe ... breathe, moon ... silver, blue ... water, we ... swim, we ... sing, we ... sing, your ... cry."

He pushed against the headache and opened his eyes to a white ceiling and the smell of alcohol or ether. He glanced around without moving his head. His head did not want to be moved. He felt bruised all over. He tried to move his mouth, to make his tongue work, to speak.

"Unh. Where ..."

Chicako's face appeared above him. "Naokisan, there you are!"

"Where ...?" he repeated as Takusan's face also moved into view.

"Koza hospital," Chicako answered. "Your head ..." She leaned in and kissed him. "So relieved ..."

"Showing off," added the other. "Yesterday, on your bike."

Other voices seemed to come from nowhere, or everywhere. "We hear, we hear, we hear, waters open. You are the second, Naokisan, the second. Snap, crackle, pop."

"The second what?" he asked aloud.

"Nothing said about second," Takusan replied. "Clowning on your bike, then the earthquake, you fell."

"So worried I have been," Chicako touched his face gently.

"The second noisemaker, Naokisan. The second. We hear, we hear, we sing. I'd like to buy the world a Coke."

"Earthquake?" he asked aloud. "You both unharmed?"

"Song, song, song, sing, sing a song," the voices in his head continued.

"A tremor only," Chicako answered. "A tremor dear one."

He closed his eyes once more and faded into sleep.

The singing continued.

Léogâne, Haiti

Samedi, 27 February 2010

Annejoule retraced her previous route toward the coast, walking more slowly now, taking further notice of the ruin lying all about. Even buildings that at first glance seemed intact showed signs of stress: cracks, sags, broken glass, wracked door frames, oddly canted roofs. Here and there a commercial building seemingly unscathed by nature appeared to have been looted: windows or doors broken out and piles of damaged goods strewn on the ground, dropped or broken in the robbers' frenzy. She passed a small backhoe, its operator caked with dust, lifting and moving bricks and timbers from one pile to another, with no obvious goal other than motion. The city's dogs, never plump, had turned more bony and wild-eyed. A few came near, but Poussez drove them off with angry barks.

They turned right onto the Chatulet road, soon bounded on both sides by makeshift camps, tents and tarps in every direction. Her heart sank. How could she ever find one person adrift in this sea of human flotsam, one single precious pebble set in kilometers of gravel roadbed? Walking more slowly still, Annejoule scanned faces from side to side, eager for familiarity that seemed nowhere evident. Most faces seemed beaten, exhausted, hungry and even desperate, while others shone with anger.

In a few places the camps seemed better organized, with clear paths laid out between rows, but most were a shambles.

Rounding a bend she came upon a crowd gathered beside a truck. Two white men were standing on the tailgate handing out strange looking tubes and speaking English. A black man was translating, talking about dirty water and how the "safe" straw made the water clean. Annejoule pressed forward and held up three fingers, "Si vous?" and was quickly handed three by a smiling worker. She examined the magic gifts briefly, then tucked them in her burlap satchel and continued up the road determined to go on with her search. But the sun was getting low now, she was hungry and weary, and the likelihood of finding her friend or even a friendly face seemed more and more remote.

A male voice near at hand interrupted her thoughts. "Hey sexy one! Hello!"

She whirled to see the boy who had threatened her soon after the quake, standing with three others in the shade of a blue tarp.

"You have something for us today?" he continued, leering and beckoning with a middle finger. "Something sweet?" The foursome started in her direction.

Annejoule backed away a few steps then turned to run, and the boys gave chase. Her bare feet hit sharp rocks as she raced along a lane, and heavy footfalls sounded behind her. Fear coursed through limbs and her breath came in gasps as she passed a last row of tents and ducked into an alley between crumbled houses. The noise behind diminished, only one pair of feet still pursuing, and then she was grabbed from behind and slammed to the ground.

The boy was instantly atop her, pulling at her clothes as

she fought back, slapping and clawing at her attacker. He hit her hard across the face. "Don't fight me. You'll make it worse." He tore at her shirt, exposing her breasts and she shoved with all her strength trying to push him away. He leaned in, tongue out, aiming for her naked skin.

Suddenly he screamed.

Poussez had dived into the melee and sunk her teeth into his arm, then pulled back, drawing blood and growling. He reached around to hit the dog and she bit again, twisting and ripping at his flesh. He halfway stood and swung again as Annejoule, now freed, kicked up hard between his legs with all of her strength and he doubled in pain, falling to his knees. Poussez dove once more, her teeth tearing his ear and barely missing an eye.

Annejoule took off running again, exhausted but too fearful to stop. Soon Poussez was loping by her side.

Koza, Japan

Nichiyōbi, 28 February 2010

When Naokisan awoke again, Chicako was seated beside his bed, reading a magazine. His head hurt less and he felt somewhat less confused. That he had fallen from his bicycle while performing a stupid stunt was clear enough, but the voices in his head had swelled and echoed through the night.

"We sing. We sing. Noisemaker Naokisan ..."

"Chicako ..."

"Feeling better?" she asked, standing and leaning in to kiss his forehead.

"Alive," he grinned, "than the alternative better is. Is today ...?"

"Nichiyōbi," she replied. "Unconscious most of yesterday you were. 'Concussion,' the doctor suggested. More the pain meds than the head bump, my guess, that knocked you out. Strange your talk has been."

"You said 'earthquake'?"

"A 7.0 quake. The Ryukyu Islands."

He could picture a map, and it seemed too distant. "Over a thousand kilometers that must be."

"A temblor here shook ... and standing on your ..."

"I know. Stupid trick."

"Impressive. Amazed I was, and the show quite enjoying, up until ..."

"Takusan?"

"Claiming school work to home he returned. Your recovery pending ... or expiration, I remain," she grinned. "Sick days from my job I obtained."

"And Oji Yam?"

"I phoned. My lie embarrassed to admit I was. Kind he was, but ..."

"So sorry I am."

"I chose to lie, with it I live. Ripples on the pond."

"For me, though ..."

"For us," she kissed him again. "Of singing you dream?"

"Strange dreams of dolphins. Singing and talking."

Ca Ira, Haiti

Dimanche, 28 February 2010

Annejoule had run much of the way back to Jeanine's shack, arriving as dusk was fading into night. She was exhausted and hungry, her heart racing as much from fear as exertion, and she'd collapsed outside the door. The old woman had come out, settled beside her and held her close as Annejoule gave way into uncontrollable sobbing. Jeanine asked no questions, and the girl finally fell asleep, her head cradled in the elder's lap.

Nor did she remember having moved inside when she awoke there Sunday morning to the sound of low voices. Jeanine was talking to a man, a realization that, at first, made the girl recoil in fear. But the male voice was calm and gentle, and it seemed clear that he must be a friend, to judge by the old woman's manner.

"So Dan-Dan, it's getting worse, not better in the city?"

"Whatever happened to your girl—you say she must have been assaulted—is common. Gangs of men and boys raping women, stealing food, taking what they wish ... they have forgotten their humanity."

"Hunger is one thing. Like salted thirst, it commands us ..."

"True enough, dear Jeanine. But what of respect? Are we no more than animals when we aren't held to account? All men have mothers. Do they imagine Maman taken in the hands of others?"

Annejoule rose and stepped outside. "Bonjou," she ventured.

"Bonjou, zanmi mwen," replied Jeanine, her eyes reflecting deep sympathy. "This is my old friend Dan-Dan Dieujuste, and this," she turned slightly, "is my new daughter, Annejoule."

"Koman ou ye?"

"J'ai été mieux," the girl replied, confused but gratified by the appelation. "Daughter," she thought but did not say. "Mother. Home. Justy." She blinked back tears.

Jeanine expanded her introduction. "Dan-Dan taught at the University of Haiti for many years in Port Au before coming home to Ca Ira. We have been friends since childhood."

"Jeanine tells me you had a bad time of it yesterday."

"A gang of boys chased me. One caught me and hit me and tore my clothes. Poussez saved me."

"Poussez?"

At mention of her name the dog had roused and ambled over to lick the girl's extended fingers. "Poussez, chen an," she said, nodding.

"Lucky to have a protector," Dan-Dan offered. "The city has become unsafe, particularly for young women. And I have it from my cousin that Port Au is worse yet. Sadly, justice is always on the side of the stronger ..."

"Which means no justice at all, and now, apparently, no laws, no restraint ..." Jeanine continued, "Our sad country has become sadder still."

"Jeanine tells me you have heard the singing of the

dolphins."

Annejoule shot a panicked glance from old man to old woman.

"Your secret is safe with Dan-Dan," Jeanine assured her. "Else I would not have shared it. Dan-Dan has heard the singing himself. As a boy he worked with his father, a long-time fisherman like my Louis. Few believe that the dauphin's sing, or else insist it is the witchy-witchy of the manbo. Best not to speak of it with others."

"I have heard the songs," came Dan-Dan's reply. "I know they sing."

"Did you understand the singing?"

"No. Only that they sang."

"I do. Or seem to. They bring me fish ..."

"So Jeanine tells me. You are special in some way, Annejoule. This is something new. Perhaps there has been some change in the dolphins' communication skills."

"Or simply that I was hit on the head." Annejoule raised her hand to her face, aching from her attacker's blow. "I've been hit quite enough, I think, to knock sense into me, or out."

Dan-Dan fixed her in a thoughtful gaze, "Whatever the cause, dear girl, it seems important. I would pay close attention if I were you. Anything is possible, and change is all around."

Kushimoto, Japan

Mokuyōbi, 4 March, 2010

Naokimat had returned to his apartment on Tuesday, evidently healthy in all respects outside of a lingering dull headache and assorted scrapes and bruises on his arms and back. Chicako had seen him home, then gone out to purchase groceries and returned to fuss over him, tucking covers around him on his futon and fixing a large bowl of miso soup.

"You will if in need call?"

"Too much already you've done," Naoki replied. "Staying at the hospital. More I could not ask."

"Less I could not have done." She kneeled to kiss his forehead. "Home now. I'd stay, but ..." the sentence dangled.

"Appearance bad," he finished her thought. "Future is." Then taking her hand, he whispered, "Marry you."

She had kissed him again and taken her leave.

As Naokimat drifted into sleep the voices, not absent since the accident, grew louder, interspersed with whistles and moans.

"We sing. We sing. Naokisan the second. The second Noisemaker. Long we have waited."

"Noisemaker?" he replied.

"You, your kind, you do not often sing. See the U.S.A. in your Chevrolet. You ride the sea on upturned islands, below the waves in hard-skinned whales. Above the waves. Below the waves. Noise. Noise. Noise. Always noise."

"Ships, we call them. Or submarines. Noise is a byproduct

of mechanical thrust."

"Ships? Submarines? Mechanical thrust? Noise Naokisan, noise. Noise to mask the singing of the singers. Noise to block the humming of the loved. Noise to block the telling of the tale."

"The tale? What tale?"

"From the beginning, Naokisan, the swimmers have swum. The singers have sung. The spinners have spun. From the beginning when the ocean was young. Krill and crab and squid and shrimp. Fish, fish, fish, fish, fish. The waters are changing, Naokisan. The singers are sad. We do not understand, Naokisan. The singers are sad."

"The second I am you say? And who is the first?"

"Annejoule. A girl. An orphan."

"Where this girl is?"

"Where the light sky is dark sky. Where Noisemakers are black. Where the water is clear. Where the dark sky is light sky. Around the great sphere."

"And did this Annejoule a blow to her head receive?"

"Shaking. Quaking. Breaking. Taking. Waking. Making. Shaking. Quaking."

"An earthquake?|

"Breaking. Taking. Shaking."

A host of other voices took up the rhyme. "Shaking. Waking. Making. Quaking. Breaking. Shaking. Taking. Shaking."

"Haiti?" Naokimat wondered aloud. It had been all over the news in January.

"We have heard the word. The word we have heard."

"Haiti, Haiti, Haiti, Haiti, Haiti," came the chorus.

"And who are you?" he thought.

"Waveweaver, I am. Waveweaver, I sing. We sing. We swim. We glide. Waveweaver, Naokisan."

"And Taiji?" he thought.

"Blood in the water. Blood on the waves." And with those words, that thought, a powerful sense of foreboding and fear. Was it simply his imagination? A welling up of his own concerns? Or could this communication be somehow real?

Naoki sighed and drifted once more into sleep. The sing-song in his head now become as gentle and comforting as a lullaby.

Ca Ira, Haiti

Lundi, 15 March 2010

In the weeks since her ill-fated foray into Léogâne, Annejoule had settled into a routine. Mornings found her at work in Jeanine's garden, weeding and picking insects off the various vegetables while Laban played nearby. The garden included cabbage, okra, tomatoes, spinach, chayote squash, eggplant, papaya, carrots, onions and more. The girl, obliged to work by her elder's generosity in room and board, was further compensated by wisdom shared.

"Ver de la tomate," Jeanine observed, holding aloft an eight centimeter long caterpillar, "Very difficult to see!" With that she pitched the hornworm beyond the garden perimeter. "But look here, Annejoule. See the chiures?" She pointed to a small pile of wet green pellets on a tomato leaf, then raised her finger several branches up the stalk to point at the culprit, it's stem-colored body all but invisible in the foliage. "Chiures easy to see."

She held the slowly writhing hornworm at face level. "These are my tomatoes!" She scolded, then tossed the pest to join its fellow outside the patch.

Bending over a squash vine where several leaves had wilted she called to Annejoule, now busily locating other tomato worms. "See this? Agrile du chayote!" Then she ran her finger down the vine to a small hole, drew a knife from her apron, and slit the stalk lengthwise. With the tip of the tool she extracted a small grey worm and tossed it aside. "My chayote, Monsieur

Agrile. Adieu!" Then she mounded dirt over the wounded stem.

Annejoule noticed days later that the vine had recovered from its wilt.

Each afternoon, while Laban napped, she and Poussez hiked to the bay shore where she settled herself in the shade of a rocky overhang, and listened.

The dolphin's communication had become more and more complex, starting with the news that she was no longer the only Noisemaker with whom contact had been established.

"Naokimat," Silver Singer had announced."Where the light sky is dark sky. Where Noisemakers are pale as the moon. Where the water is green. Where the dark sky is light sky."

"Naokimat is a name? It seems strange."

"Naokimat. Naokisan. All names are strange, all names may change. Singing we sing. Bringing we bring. The ocean is changing, we don't understand."

"What is changing, Silver Singer?"

"The taste. The clam. The fish. The shrimp. The waves. The wind. The ocean we have known since the beginning is an ocean we don't now know."

"When was the beginning, Silver Singer?"

"In the borning in the morning, in the morning when we swam."

"Do you mean today?"

"What is today, Annejoule? What do you mean by today?"

"This day. Eight hours ago the sun rose on this day. In a few more it will set."

"What is this day, Annejoule. What are hours? Ever we

have swum, from light to dark to light to dark, from storm to calm to storm to calm. Ever we have swum since the borning in the morning."

"Days run from dawn to dawn," Annejoule explained. "Each light time is different."

"Light and dark are always and ever, Annejoule. Ever the light is bright, sweeping the sea. Light here, dark there, light there, dark here. In the morning swam my mother's mother's mother, and hers before and hers before, back and back to the bringing of the light. Choosey mothers choose Jif. Ever we have swum, ever will we swim. Measuring light to light, you speak of days, Annejoule, but light is. Ever and always, light is. You speak of days, Annejoule, but there is only one borning, one morning, one swimming we've swum."

Annejoule frowned. The notion that there had only ever been one day seemed strange in the extreme. She counted her own life in days and months and years, almost 17 of them. "How old are you, Silver Singer?"

"What do you mean? What is old?"

"How many years since you were born?"

"What are years, Annejoule?"

The girl thought back to school lessons, searching for an explanation. "A year is the time it takes for the earth to go around the sun."

"Mystery upon mystery, Annejoule. What is time? What is the earth? The sun at least I know."

"Time ..." she began, then realized that the idea of time was exactly the concept she couldn't describe. "I'll start with the sun," she continued, "You know the sun is the bright, hot, round thing in the sky, like the moon, which you sing about, only brighter. It comes up every morning and goes down in the evening."

"You speak of the sun but the sun is unlike the moon," Silver Singer replied. "The moon changes while the sun is the same. There is the light and the dark, the brightening and the dimming. The moon comes and goes, ever changing like the sea. Since the borning in the morning the sunlight has waxed and waned. The moon has glowed and changed. But up is where we breathe and down is where we dine. Up and down, do the sun and moon breathe and dine?"

"The sun doesn't really go up and down. It just looks that way because the earth is turning."

"And what is this earth you speak of?"

"It is the planet we live on. A ball that moves through space. It goes around the sun."

"Planet? Ball? Space? These are Noisemaker things?"

"No. You live on the planet earth as well."

"Then why do we not know of this thing? We swim, we swim, we swim. Up we breathe and down we dine. Squiddiddy. Squiddiddish. Squiddeamish. Fish. Fish. Fish. Fish. Fish. Things go better with Coke. Tell me, Annejoule, why does this earth you speak of go around the sun you have described?"

"There is something called gravity. It's what keeps us on earth. It's the thing that lets us feel our weight."

"Weight? What is weight, Annejoule? Another Noise-maker mystery?"

"Weight is what makes you fall back into the water when you leap into the air."

"No, dear girl. That isn't weight. It is love."

Annejoule considered the statement and discovered it made quite as much sense as her teacher's explanation for gravity, then let it go. "How do you know about the other Noisemaker. Did you call him Naokisan?"

"Naokimat. Naokisan. Naoki."

"Does he know you have contacted me?"

"Ever we have waited, Annejoule. Joyous we sing."

"Can you tell him 'Hello from Haiti'?"

"Hello. Hello. Hello."

Kushimoto, Japan

Mokuyōbi, 18 March, 2010

As he awakened, Naoki experienced the strongest communication yet from the dolphin, Waveweaver.

"Hello. Hello. Hello. Hello from Haiti."

"From Haiti?"

"From the Noisemaker Annejoule. 'Hello from Haiti.' Annejoule speaks of Noisemaker mysteries we do not understand. 'Time,' she says, and 'years,' and 'gravity,' and 'weight,' so many mysteries that make no sense. Do you share such mysteries, Naokimat?"

"None of those are mysteries to me, Waveweaver. They are commonplace." He thought for a moment then explained, "Time is the measured or measurable period during which an action, process, or condition exists or continues. A year is ..."

Waveweaver interrupted, "What is this thing you call measured?"

"To measure is ..." he hesitated. "A measure is a standard used for determining the dimensions, area, volume, or weight of something."

"More mysteries, Naokimat. Weight, what is weight? Annejoule speaks of weight as well."

Naoki shook his head. He was fully awake now and abruptly recognized the gap in understanding. How could he explain weight to a creature that existed in weightlessness? Measurement to a creature without technology? All of his referents were clearly technological at their base. Would a cetacean have any need of counting? Of counting anything at all?

"How often do you breathe?" he asked.

"We breathe when we breathe. We sing when we sing. We swim when we swim. We eat when we eat. Winston tastes good like a cigarette should."

"Noisemakers would say that you breathe every eight or ten minutes."

"Minutes? Eight? Minutes. Minutes. Ten. Minutes." It seemed that a whole chorus of voices had chimed in, with the words overlapping in quick succession, some repeating as a statement, others questioning. "Minutes? Minutes. Ten? Eight. Minutes. Minutes? Eight? Minutes. Ten? Minutes. Minutes? We breathe when we breathe. Eight?" It sounded like utter nonsense, and Naoki experienced a deeper realization, that number itself had to be meaningless to nontechnological creatures. "We breathe when we breathe."

"Conveying a message to Annejoule is possible? Hello from Japan. It seems we are experiencing a very strange phenomenon. Are you a scientist?"

"Hello. Hello. Hello. Hello Annejoule, from Japan."

Ca Ira, Haiti

Samedi, 21 March 2010

Annejoule considered the difference between her own and Silver Singer's thoughts and how very different the world would seem to creatures immersed in the ocean. She shed her clothes and waded out into the bay, swimming and then floating on her back. "This is weightless," she mused.

"We swim! We swim! We swim!" continued in the background of her thoughts.

Later, she was sitting beneath her shelter rock when Silver Singer delivered a message. "Hello from Japan. It seems we are experiencing a very strange phenomenon. Are you a scientist?"

"Hello, Silver Singer. Is this greeting from Naoki?"

"Naokimat. Naokisan. Naoki. Naoki. This message is for Annejoule from Naoki. Strange words. Strange ideas. What is a scientist, Annejoule. Are you a scientist?"

She laughed aloud at the notion. "Non! Not a chance! I am just a young woman, a girl, with some little bit of education and no chance of getting more. Scientists attend school for many years, and go to university. They know many more things than this poor girl."

"Whatever these 'scientists' may know, and whatever these 'years' are that you speak of, none have communicated with us as you have. Only you and Naoki."

"You told me the ocean is changing. What do you mean when you say that? What is changing?"

"Ice melting. Krill dying. Squid missing. Eels reeling. Great currents running muddy and fish; fish flee. Jellyfish. Jellyfish. Jellyfish. Jellyfish."

"When did the changes start?"

"Change is change is change. Changes happen when changes happen. The ocean is changing."

It quickly struck Annejoule that the question of "when?" involved time, so she altered course. "Where are these changes happening?"

"Here in the turquoise sea. There in the green sea. Off in the grey sea. Over in the blue sea. Under the deep sea. Beyond the far sea. Deep in the cold sea. Below the ice. In light and in dark."

"And how do these changes feel, Silver Singer? How do they affect you?"

"The ocean is lonely. Swimmy swimmers swim alone. Jellyfish. Jellyfish. Jellyfish. Jellyfish."

"There are many jellyfish?" Annejoule wondered, half aloud.

"Jellyfish. Jellyfish. Jellyfish. Jellyfish." came the reply. "And new noisemaker noise. Loud noisemaker noise. Noise to make the swimmy swimmers scream in pain. Noise to make the swimmy swimmers leave the mother ocean. One banana, two banana, three banana, four.

Kushimoto, Japan

Nichiyōbi, 28 March, 2010

"Dreams they do not seem to be." Naokimat sat on the sand beside Chicako in their cove. He was attempting to describe his experience of the past three weeks, still not entirely sure that any of it made sense.

"Most frequently the dolphin Waveweaver I hear. Her thoughts or her voice. A human girl in Haiti, she, and I think it is a 'she' describes. Another with whom the dolphins contact have made."

"And bumping your head not the cause?"

"That was the start, but ..."

"We sing. We sing. We sing. Naokisan we sing your name!"

"I'm hearing it now," he said.

"Saying?" Chicako sounded skeptical.

"They sing. They sing. Near at hand they seem."

"Here now to come, Waveweaver, you might request? Near to come," the girl suggested.

"On the shore, high rocks between, I am," he said aloud, and thought. "Here the cove within. Can you me find?"

Minutes passed and Naoki shook his head. "Perhaps not. I know not. Strange it all seems."

"Badly banged up you were. And complex the brain ..."

Suddenly a pod of dolphins appeared at the cove's mouth. Two came on ahead of the others, quite close to shore, an adult and one much smaller. The larger approached and tipped an eye out of the water. "Waveweaver I am," she thought at Naoki. "Naokisan are you."

Chicako gripped Naoki's arm and stared, but her boyfriend pulled away, waded into the waves and stroked the dolphin's side. "Naokisan I am."

"And this my daughter, Surfslider."

As the pod swam back toward open water, Naoki turned and locked eyes with Chicako, who nodded in affirmation.

"And Taiji, when I mention, bloody water the only answer. There soon I need to go."

"Not alone," came her quick reply. "Not alone."

Kushimoto, Japan

Kayōbi, 30 March, 2010

Naoki bowed as he entered the small, spare office, a gesture returned by his oceanography adviser, Koichi Sekiguchi.

"Honored professor, troubled by a story concerning dolphins I am."

"Yes."

"Japanese fishermen, informed I am, dolphins in great numbers slaughter. In Taiji."

"Rumors the internet spawns. By officials in Taiji denounced. As you know, Mr. Matsumoto, *Delphinus capensis, Delphinus delphis* nor *Delphinus tropicalis* do our people consume. Neither *Stenella longirostris* a dietary item for Japanese constitute . Pointless such slaughter would be."

"Yet, of a film I have heard, in North America shown ..."

"Critically considered all such rumors must upon hearing be. Examinations soon, sir. Studying I'd suggest. No nonsense rumors the internet from to repeat." Koichi nodded dismissively.

Bowing, Naoki backed out of the room. "For consideration you I thank."

As he walked down the dim hallway the voices resumed in his head. "Blood in the water. Blood on the waves. J'ai ton amour, I don't wanna be friends. I want your bad romance. Sing, we sing, we sing." Then, suddenly, he experienced the sensation of water rushing over his skin. Somewhat disoriented, he leaned against the wall and closed his eyes.

All around him he saw myriad glistening fish, a school darting and weaving in a synchronized swim. To his right and below he could see three dolphins in full pursuit.

"Waveweaver I am. Fish, fish, fish, fish, fish. Pepsi Cola hits the spot."

He opened his eyes, steadied himself with a deep breath, and continued on his way.

Ca Ira, Haiti

Mercredi, 31 March 2010

"Dan-Dan, the dolphins say the ocean has changed, is changing. Do you know of this?" The girl had followed a dirt track to a shallow ford in La Rouyonne, crossed the river, and continued toward the village of Ca Ira. Jeanine had told her that Dan-Dan's was the second house along the way.

"Ah, Annejoule, that is clearly the case. For example, there are far more jellyfish in the bay than just ten years past." The elder continued digging the post hole he'd been working when his visitor arrived. "And the fish in the village nets are much smaller," he added.

"The dolphins don't seem to understand numbers, but they sing jellyfish, jellyfish, jellyfish, jellyfish. Do you have some idea why the sea would change? She is so ancient. Doesn't Agwe protect her ocean?"

The old man hesitated before answering. He put down his shovel and motioned for Annejoule to join him in the shade of his porch roof. He settled on a weathered wooden stool. "Come, sit." He gestured to another stool.

"You are young. I am old, and not eager to challenge the things taught by your mother, by others. But you are somehow special. You have been called to something very large. Very important. Many fishermen have heard the dolphin's singing. But never with understanding. Myself, I would have been inclined to the belief that it was all in your imagination."

Annejoule started to protest, but he raised his palm and padded the air, a clear invocation to silence.

"But they bring you fish. You are clearly, clearly hearing their call, their meaning, and they are clearly hearing yours in return. I have never, in a long life, heard of such a thing. Never read of it in books. Never heard of it at the university. You are special Annejoule, and so I will speak to you as an adult."

"Agwe does not protect the ocean," he continued. "Agwe, it seems to me, does not exist at all."

They sat silent for long minutes as Annejoule considered the implications of his statement. She finally replied, "Nor Damballa? Nor Bondye?"

Dan-Dan shook his head.

"And no Guinee?"

Dan-Dan splayed his hands, palms up, and shrugged.

"Nor the Christian god spoken of in churches?"

"I think not. What god would visit her creation with disease? What god would crush poor and hungry people with earthquakes and drown them with hurricanes? What god would ignore the prayers of the sick and the dying? Our fate, it seems to me, is up to us."

"Oh, Dan-Dan. That seems so strange. Against all I've been told all my life. Surely so many people cannot be so very wrong."

"That troubled me for many years, my dear girl. Many years. Nor do others like to hear such views expressed. Even Jeanine, my oldest and dearest friend, covers her ears if I mention these thoughts. And yet, no other explanation makes sense to me.

Life is too random, too full of happenstance to be directed by invisible gods. If they are so unimaginably stupid or sloppy or cruel, what would be their qualifications for deity?" Dan-Dan shook his head. "But I'll tell you what. Did not the dolphins tell you that you are the first?"

"That's true. And now a second, in Japan."

"Not much contact yet with us humans, then. Ask your ocean friends if they know Agwe, or Damballa, or Simbi or any of the others. Surely creatures of the ocean would know more of ocean gods than we two-leggeds on land!"

Annejoule nodded thoughtfully, then rose and picked up Dan-Dan's shovel and continued her friend's task in silence. She punched the shovel deep into the sandy soil, as her thoughts turned to her Maman and Justy. She'd searched and searched to find reasons for their demise. Perhaps there was no reason to be found.

Later, when Dan-Dan thanked her for the help, he added a question. "Before the quake, were you in school?"

"A little. But Maman needed my help ..." she trailed off.

"Can you read?"

"Yes," and then, a little taken aback, "Of course!"

"Would you like to take up your lessons again?"

"I will never have the money."

"But it appears you have the time."

"That's true."

"Come back tomorrow afternoon," he smiled and patted her shoulder. "I have missed teaching these past few years. I would very much enjoy having a student once again."

"What will I study? There is so very much I do not know."

"I think we'll start with questions. What would you like to know, Annejoule?"

Walking back to Jeanine's home, Annejoule experienced a feeling of deep reflief. She'd seen her mother's death as punishment, perhaps for her Maman, perhaps for herself. She'd wondered what she'd done to anger the gods or God, what prayer or ritual her mother had failed to perform, why innocent little Justinien had been taken from this life, or taken from her own. She had felt guilt in her survival, asking "Why Maman? Why not me?"

But maybe there were no gods to appease, no gods in control, therefore no cause for guilt, no reason beyond chance. Not even fate. There remained only today and yesterday and tomorrow. If there were no gods out there somewhere dictating what she could do or be or become, then there were no insurmountable limits at all.

And, yet, if there were no gods and no heaven, was there any reason whatever for hope? Would it always and ever be pain and loss and memory of those missing?

School, she thought. School. What would she become if there were no limits? What in all the world would she like to know?

Kushimoto, Japan

Kinyōbi, 2 April, 2010

"Koichi dismissed it out of hand."

Takusan nodded and replied, "But Naokisan, the link I sent on, the clip you watched?"

"And the Web sites I visited. But the internet a hall of mirrors comprises."

"The video ...?"

"Yes Takusan. But telling you more I must be. Voices heard, within my brain."

"To your spill consequent?"

"Yes."

"Telling you?"

"Trusting of you in not sharing with others I am ."

"Friends for so long being ?"

"Friends in truth. Takusan, with dolphins communicating I am."

Takusan, straddling his bicycle leaned forward on the handle bars. "The doctors you have asked? Concussion is ..."

"Calling, they come."

"The voices?"

"The dolphins."

"With difficulty believing. But ... yes, believing."

"Two hours you can spare?" Naoki queried his friend, and receiving nodded assent he added, "Follow me."

Peddling hard the pair sped down the coast road south, to

the pebble-strewn path that led to the lovers' quiet cove."

"Voices of Taiji you are telling? Of slaughter?"

Naoki replied, "All I know, telling will follow. Showing first." He continued to lead his friend to a rocky promontory that fell sharply to the gently churning water. They sat together and looked out over a quiet, calm ocean.

"High tide, or nearly," Takusan observed.

"Now, I call. Waveweaver, here I am." His voice was low.

"Hearing difficult, I think," said Takusan. "You softly speak."

"For you. Mind to mind the dolphins connect. And at times the water I can feel. Other dolphins I can see."

The pair sat in silence for a quarter of an hour and then fins appeared at the entrance to the cove. Naoki nodded, glancing at his companion.

"Coincidence possible. Dolphins the coastal waters inhabit."

One fin moved shoreward from the pod, its owner bolting from the water in two arcing leaps, then disappearing beneath the surface only to reappear at the foot of the rock. The dolphin canted sideways, eyeing the two young men, head above the water.

"Waveweaver, this is Takusan."

The dolphin squeaked and clicked, then dove again.

"Takusan knows of Taiji," Naoki intoned.

The dolphin exploded from the waves in a series of leaps, each ending on its back. It then reappeared below the rock and rolled upside down, floating still as death for several long minutes.

"Waveweaver what tells? Saying she is?"

"Help us. Help us. Help us. We sing. We sing. We sing."

"A journal dear friend you'd best be keeping."

Ca Ira, Haiti

Dimanche, 4 April 2010

Annejoule sat quietly beneath the rock shelf on the shore and directed her thoughts toward Silver Singer. "I have a question. Can you answer? Oh my friend can you answer?"

Multiple voices responded. "Singing we are. Singing we swim. Pepsi Cola hits the spot. Fish, fish, fish, fish."

"Silver Singer do you know of Agwe?"

"Agwe the noisemakers say. Noisemakers with nets say Agwe, Agwe, Agwe."

"Do you know that Agwe is a spirit?"

"Agwe is a noise noisemakers make. Annejoule, Annejoule, what is a spirit? Can you sing me the song of a spirit?

"No, I've never heard one.."

"Silver Singer has never heard one either. Have you seen one Annejoule?"

"No."

"What then do these spirits do?"

"Agwe protects fish, she is the spirit of fish and seaweed."

"Not from me! Fish, fish, fish, fish. The spirit of fish tastes good!" In the squeals and squeaks that followed Annejoule got the strong impression that dozens of dolphins were laughing as she continued. "And if this Agwe cannot be seen, where would we not see her?"

"Agwe lives in Ville au Camp, a city deep beneath the waves."

"What is a city?"

"A city is a place where many noisemakers live."

"But noisemakers cannot live beneath the waves. Like dolphins you must breathe or die. So Agwe lives where no noisemaker can live, and where no dolphin can visit for long. 'Agwe, Agwe' is spoken by noisemakers with nets, but Agwe cannot be heard or seen. And Agwe protects the fish unless I am hungry. A very strange thing this spirit."

"Actually, Ville au Camp is said to be the city where noisemaker spirits go after they die."

"It's good that they die first, because otherwise they would drown. But what is a spirit?"

"It's the invisible part of a noisemaker, or I suppose a dolphin, or any other living thing, that keeps living after one dies."

"Living is living, Annejoule. And dying is dying. Or so it seems to me."

Annejoule thought a moment and said, "Agwe is a loa. A loa works with Bondye the creator."

"What is a creator Annejoule? You speak of many strange things."

"It is said that Bondye made the earth."

"Ah, the earth again. You say we all live on the earth. But the earth is another thing Silver Singer has never heard or seen. We live. We live. We sing. We sing. Since the beginning we have swum. Since the beginning we have breathed. Billie Jean is not my lover."

"But what came before the beginning?" Annejoule

wondered.

"Nothing," answered Silver Singer. "Nothing began until everything had begun. And we swim and we've swum. Plop, plop. Fizz, fizz."

"Why do you sing so many nonsense words, Silver Singer? You sing of Pepsi and Coke and cigarettes and medicine."

"We have learned the words of noisemakers, the songs sung on noisemaker boats. We have learned your songs to communicate with you. Songs repeated often must be important. We sing the songs of our ancestors and we sing the songs of yours. We have repeated your songs again and again to try to connect. But you are the first, Annejoule. And Naoki the second."

That made sense. The dolphins heard the sounds of radios on fishing boats.

Silver Singer broke into her thoughts again." We sing the songs we have always sung. We tell the tale we have always told. And this Agwe seems utterly absent. I just caught another snapper. Are you hungry?"

"Yes, quite hungry," thought Annejoule. "And I am happy you are my benefactor."

Soon two dolphins swam close to shore and Annejoule, grinning, scooped up two fresh fish.

"Thank you my friends."

"Squiddish, squidapple, squideemish. We sing and swim and sing. You deserve a break today. Just beat it. Just beat it."

Kushimoto, Japan

Doyōbi, 10 April, 2010

"On your seat today you will stand?" Chicako grinned at her boyfriend.

"Likely not."

"Earthquakes from today's weather report are absent," jibed Takusan. "Bicycle tricks okay."

"This round chances not taken ..."

"This round, from Ojisan permission sought and granted. In truth my heart rejoices."

"Overnight?"

"Himself once young. In truth more trust."

Then they were off, following the Kumano Highway through Kihime, past Koza, then inland from Kitahara where steep hills had the threesome puffing and dripping. Spring wildflowers lined their route, and in some stretches drifting traces of honeysuckle were carried on the breeze. They paused for lunch in a wooded stretch, bikes tipped against blossoming trees, before heading downhill to the seaside once more.

"The plan?" Takusan inquired.

"In revelation authorities have no interest. Others, our age meeting. Questions indirect, text connections conversation to continue. Low key," Naoki offered. "Very low key."

"And photos?" Chicako suggested.

"Photos. Tourists snap photos. We tourists are."

Soon they were riding along the harbor at Uragami.

Leaving town, the road stayed close to the water and a steady seabreeze kept the riders cool. Vehicle traffic was heavier now, and after several more kilometers, Naoki turned off the highway to follow a less hazardous route through Konoshiro and Yatagano. They crossed the long bridge into Shimosato, crossed more low hills and soon made their way through city streets and found themselves beside the harbor in Taiji.

A tall statue of a smiling dolphin stood not far from the water, and Chicako snapped pictures.

"Internet cafe?" asked Takusan. "Or a college?"

"Neither." Naoki displayed an area map on his iPhone. "Young people perhaps at sports field, here." He pointed at a section near the bay. "Perhaps at Hiromitsu Ochiai Baseball Museum. Art museum a possibility."

"The famous cove where located?" Chicako inquired.

"North of town, the national park within."

"Out then fanning? Again at two, here meet?" Takusan suggested.

"Sports field for me," Chicako offered.

Takusan claimed the "Baseball museum."

"To the infamous cove later we can ride," observed Naoki. Then the conspirators parted to pursue new friends and, hopefully, informants.

When the trio reconvened Takusan was ebullient. "Long ago a visit here was called for. Hiromitsu Ochiai my hero since childhood. Oreryu his style and mine."

"Possession of style not immediately apparent," jibed Naoki.

"Famous moments video and photos display. Bats and gloves, pennants and trophies," continued the young fan. "Heaven to a fan."

"Likely sources you met?" Chicako inquired.

"Away from me the time sped ..." he shrugged as his friends laughed aloud. "Wise man one time in thousand a mistake makes, too," he continued, repeating the aphorism with a nodding bow.

"Possession of wisdom not immediately apparent," Naoki added. "And you, Chicako?"

The girl blinked and offered a coy smile. "Phone numbers exchanged with eight young men, very attractive." Seeing Naoki's disgruntled look, she gestured and added "About this tall, with fewer clothes ..." obviously amused at her repetition of his private joke. "Swimming team members, all eight, and three young women. Basketball for an hour or so we played."

"And of dolphins ...?"

"Conversation with the swimmers made easier. Pride evident positive comparison to finned mammals following. Shoichi the name of one among them." She tipped her phone to display a photo of a grinning, muscular athlete in a Speedo. "When per Taiji fame for dolphins observation made, Shoichi said, 'The one who swims can sink.' Parting he urged, 'Call me.' Arched eyes in dolphin situation suggested, not Chicako, his interest."

Naoki nodded thoughtfully. "Good that is."

"The last?"

He laughed, "That too! But reflected in his comment

knowing. Art museum closed. New exhibit mounting. To the jetty I biked. Fishing folk in dozens, and a few befriended. One very attractive woman, about this tall ..." he laughed with Chicako, while Takusan looked bewildered. "Private joke," explained his friend. "Anti-dolphin most talk. Competition for fish, they claimed. Shoichi our best contact so far."

"Also in the harbor, cages. Fins cresting. Dolphins there. Sale to American and European marine parks by jetty informants indicated."

With that the threesome started on the road east and north from Taiji.

Ca Ira, Haiti

Samedi, 10 April 2010

Annejoule had begun her lessons with what seemed to be a basic question.

"Even before the earthquake, life was hard," she had started. "Life was difficult for everyone in Léogâne. My family was poorer than some, better off than many. Mother worked hard selling flowers, and I helped. Yet there were men in long cars, there were mansions on the hilltops, there were posters in shops with pictures of Americans who I think must be very rich. Life did not look hard for those people. I often wondered if they ever worked and why we were never more than a few days from hunger. Why are we so poor?"

Dan-Dan laughed, "A very good question, indeed!" He paused and stroked his chin. "Or more than one question. What you are asking is 'Why are so many in Haiti poor?' Or perhaps, 'Why is Haiti, as a nation, poor?' And that is a very big question, requiring a very long answer."

He had given Annejoule a book titled *A propos de l'histoire d'Haiti, saviez-vous que,* warning that while it was only one writer's viewpoint, the views were well informed. He handed over a dictionary as well, noting that she might find unfamiliar words in the text. Annejoule had then read in fascination a history of her world. Her questions had branched out, examining slavery and revolution, leadership and subjugation.

"But we have been a democracy for many years now, how

is it that we are still so poor?"

"Democracy is sometimes more apparent than real," came Dan-Dan's reply. "Jeanine is one of the wisest people I have ever met, but the chance that she would ever be elected president of Haiti is less than zero. The wealthy divide power amongst themselves, and so it is one wealthy faction or another that exerts real power, no matter what the people might want to decide."

"And so there is no hope?" Annejoule sighed.

"What hope there is resides at the very local level. We can help each other, as Jeanine has helped you and you me."

"Perhaps we can help others ...?" The girl trailed off.

"Perhaps," came her mentor's reply. "

Taiji, Japan

Doyōbi, 10 April, 2010

Evening approached as the trio arrived at the storied cove. The anticipated guards did not materialize and they faced no obstruction in their descent to the shore, a scene of cascading rocky cliffs and gentle surf.

"Not now, the season for capture," observed Takusan. "Dolphins in September driven."

"A lovely place," added Chicako.

"Yes. Of horror at other times, water red running, but now, lovely," rejoined Naoki.

With nothing to observe beyond the waves and wind and sand, the friends lingered awhile on the shore, then headed upslope to a quiet glen where they opened bentos to eat sticky rice, pickles and fish, then stretched out sleeping pads for the night.

As they lay back Chicako asked, "How many?"

"Dolphins? Killed?" Takusan answered, "Hundreds, thousands, difficult knowing is. Marine parks the young ones, alive purchase. Others eaten are."

"Who would?"

"Whale meat labeled it is."

"Few enough whale today eat."

"Butchers a market find."

"Creatures of great beauty ..."

"And intelligence."

"To me now they sing," Naokisan interjected, breaking his silence.

"Of what?" Chicako spoke quietly.

"Usual singsong, serious with jingles mixed. 'Fish, fish, fish, fish, fish' a constant theme. 'Things go better with Coke. Help us!' one inveighs. Singing their whole lives. To my mind only occasional breakthroughs. Seeming so.

"This too. The Haitian, Annejoule, her thoughts sometimes ..."

"You hear them?"

"Perhaps. Traces of thoughts. Haitian history. The name Dan-Dan recurs. A teacher, I think."

Ca Ira, Haiti

Jeudi, 15 April 2010

"Poussez has been scratching a lot, poor girl."

Jeanine squatted beside the dog and parted her fur with weathered fingers. "Fleas," she announced. "Annejoule, there are plants along the far edge of the garden, dusty green with lobed leaves. If you tear a leaf the smell is quite pungent, you'll know you have the right one. Fetch a handful of leaves and we'll fix Poussez's troubles."

Soon enough the task was accomplished, and the pup seemed to enjoy being rubbed all over with the repellent greens.

"Jeanine, how did you learn all you know about plants?"

"Jeanine is a very old woman, my dear one. I have had a great many years to watch, and listen, and remember. Damballa has been good to me."

Annejoule considered her conversations with Dan-Dan concerning the Haitian gods and Jeanine's displeasure in hearing them challenged and decided discretion was the wiser course. "Have you always grown so many vegetables and medicines?" she asked.

"As a young wife Jeanine knew only a little that Maman had shown me. But I had long times alone when Louis was off to sea. Time to listen and watch. Damballa showed me new plants, Damballa walked me into another village. Damballa wanted Jeanine to learn how green things grow. So I learned a little at a time and each by each I grew to know more."

"You've taught me a bit, just working beside you in the garden. But I'd like to know more, Jeanine. Will you teach me?"

The older woman smiled and flung her arms wide. "Teachers are everywhere. The seed tells us how deep to plant by its size. The plant tells us how it wants to grow. The fruit tells us when to be picked by its color. And the birds and the bugs and the mice and the snakes each tell a tale of their purpose. Damballa has told all creation to teach us its ways."

"They don't talk to me," observed Annejoule, frowning.

"They talk, my dear one, but you don't yet know how to listen. That, I might teach you. In return, can you teach me to hear the dauphin?"

"If I could. But it is not something I learned. It simply happened. Perhaps, if my understanding grows ..."

And so a more formal schooling had begun, with garden work and lessons in the mornings, and more formal lessons from Dan-Dan in the afternoon. All the while Annejoule was thinking about how she might use her new knowledge to help her battered community and the dolphins who, more and more, were present in her mind.

"Fish, fish, fish, fish. Food, food, food, food, food," they sang. "You deserve a break today, at McDonald's."

Kushimoto, Japan

Doyōbi, 17 April, 2010

"Taijian mercury levels tested, you have heard?" asked Chicako.

Naoki pressed his cell phone closer to his ear. "No. What's up?"

"In Taiji, Shoichi, our friend, a study reports."

Naoki, recalling the swimmer's photo, fought off a flash of jealousy. "A study?"

"In Taiji, blood mercury levels of the people extremely high. Only plausible cause high level predator species-consumption."

"Dolphin meat also tested?"

"Results confirmed."

"Local marine mammal consumption therefore surely widespread."

"So it seems."

"He the report can send?"

"Expecting."

"You I tomorrow can see? You Chicako I dearly love."

"And you," she replied. "At two?"

"Soon enough it is not," he answered as they ended the conversation.

Naoki relayed the news to Takusan, who was ebullient. "See! The stories confirmed. Koichi what now says?"

Ca Ira, Haiti

Jeudi, 22 April 2010

Annejoule carefully cut stems from a manioc bush with her mother's knife, removed the leaves and delivered them to Jeanine for planting. The older woman had explained, "With you to help, we can grow much more than Jeanine could alone. We will have manioc to sell next year."

Dan-Dan appeared in the garden shortly before noon, looking agitated. "News," he intoned. "Very bad news." His face was grim. "For the dolphins."

Annejoule started. "News for the dolphins? What do you mean?"

The trio joined Laban in the shade of clump of palms and sat as Jeanine queried, "Tell us. What news?"

"My brother, Fedji, in Miami, phoned."

Annejoule started again. Dan-Dan had a phone? But, of course, he'd been at the university and his home had electric lights. Still ...

"There has been an explosion of an oil well in the Gulf of Mexico. Oil is pouring out. It cannot be stopped. Oil and more oil poisoning the water. The dolphins must be warned."

"Your brother?" Annejoule asked. "In Miami?"

"Teaching at the university there. A chemist."

"You have a phone?" came her next question, feeling a little stupified. "I mean, of course, your brother telephoned. But an explosion? Oil?"

"There is so much to explain, and I have very little information to share. But many thousands of liters of oil are pouring out into the sea. The dolphins must be warned away. They will die."

"Wouldn't they be the first to know?" Jeanine queried. "After all they are in the water."

"By the time they taste it, it could be too late. Annejoule, please tell them."

"I will, Dan-Dan. Immediately. I will."

The girl rose, and followed by Poussez, loped toward her cavern on the shore. Even before she reached the listening post she had connected with Silver Singer.

"Danger," she warned, "Extreme danger. Poison. Black poison. Tell others. Swim away."

Silver Singer replied, "Away from?"

The girl paused. How to explain directions in a directionless sea? She had little enough grasp of where the explosion had occured, even of where exactly the ocean called the Gulf of Mexico began or ended. Even describing it to herself seemed muddled. Further, the idea of learning about the event via a telephone call was muddled. She'd never held a phone, though she'd seen many in the hands of rich tourists in Léogâne. She'd no idea that Dan-Dan owned one.

She thought hard about direction. "Toward me," she replied. "Toward where light first arrives after dark. Away from a terrible explosion. Some among you must have heard."

The dolphin was briefly silent, then, "Sisters and brothers in the blue green sea sing of great noise. They sing of billowing blackness. They sing of fish easily eaten, slow swimming in circles Slow squid easily eaten. Feasting they are."

"Swim away from the slow fish!" Annejoule shouted aloud. "Poison. Bad. Away! Away!"

"I will sing to my sisters. Sing to my brothers. See the USA in your Chevrolet!"

The dolphin veered off into singsong and another voice intruded. "Annejoule, what has happened? This is Naoki."

"An explosion in the Gulf of Mexico. An oil well."

"A disaster," came his reply, and then silence.

Kushimoto, Japan

Kinyōbi, 23 April, 2010

Chicako and Naoki sat on the wharf, a short walk from Oji Yam's boatyard, discussing what they'd heard concerning the BP oil blowout, now and then holding hands and enjoying the bright day despite the grim news half a world away.

"But for me," the boy observed, "Personally. Communication from Annejoule so amazingly clear."

"Distressed, she was," Chicako suggested.

"Very. Thought clear as speech. As if across a table from me sitting. 'An explosion the Gulf of Mexico within.' Oddly in Japanese understood, yet in what manner expressed, French? Creole? Thoughts an accent might have?"

"The American linguist, Pinker, of language instinct wrote. Universal mentalese. Chomsky as well. But from lectures, specifics I cannot recall. Language course you also took. Thought translingual ...?"

"And transpecial? The professor laughing aloud I now hear." Naoki shook his head. Then, nodding, "I the dolphins daily better comprehend. Yet, also, their songs with advertising and pop songs constantly, confusingly interlaced. Intelligent they seem ..."

"To dolphin thought the theories of Noam Chomsky apply?"

"Could be. Linguists evidence of cetacean syntax now confirm. Killer whales the north Pacific inhabiting from others in north Atlantic in dialect differing. Dolphins each other by name identifying. Humpback songs through generations singing."

"This the proof of sentience. Proof for protection needed. Thoughts of public going?"

"Who believing? Naokisan, to cycling accident pursuant, talking dolphins hears? Likely not."

"Annejoule as well ..."

"Ah, yes. Naokisan also the voice of Haitian earthquake victim now hearing. Address please? Full name? Credentials?"

"The dolphins Annejoule was warning?"

"So it seemed. Clear the warning was. Less clear other thoughts. The very idea of a telephone seemed to her confusing. Or to the dolphins? Sensible that would be. Annejoule's thoughts I hear, or Annejoule's thoughts as dolphins think them?"

Chicako laughed, "Telepaths telephones need not!" Then, shyly, "Your thoughts I sometimes wish I'd hear."

"Telepathy from mind reading differs. Messaging volitional. If you my mind could however read, my honesty you'd discover. You I love," he leaned in to kiss her shoulder.

"Both ways mind reading could cut." She laughed again, scooting away. "Me naked in your imagination, and what more?"

"That a dream was."

"A dream remembered?"

"Happily. But your photo of Shoi ..."

"Of him naked I have not dreamed ..." she insisted. Then looked up, pursed her lips, and grinned, "At least, not yet."

Naoki's eyes widened in mock shock though his expression belied real dismay. He lunged, reaching, as if to grab his fiance's hand but Chicako jumped up and skipped down the dock, laughing. "Jealous! Jealous you are!"

He hurried after her. "Chako, uncertainty difficult is."

She turned, laughing, and thrust her hips suggestively and ventured, "Heisenberg forgetting?"

Ca Ira, Haiti

Mercedi, 27 April 2010

"It's strange to hear stories from Dan-Dan's brother, in a distant place about events more distant still. Every bit of my life has changed since ..." Annejoule glanced up from her weeding.

Jeanine paused in her own task and sighed. "Ah, child, when you reach my age you'll know. Agwe brings change, always change."

"But before ..." the girl bit her lip. "Before, with Maman and Justy, each day was much the same. And since ..."

"Agwe is one of many. Some days, some seasons, some years, the changes come from this loa or that loa. Bondye knows. Jeanine only listens. Agwe or Damballa must have special interest in you, my daughter. You alone hear the spinners singing and understand."

Spotting a hornworm on a branch between them, Jeanine reached over and plucked it from the tomato stem. "There's much that changes not at all. Ver de la tomate," she laughed as she pitched the squirming invader over the fence. "Will be in your tomatoes long after Jeanine joins Louis below the sea."

The pair worked in silence a while longer, then Dan-Dan strode into the garden. His expression was grim and his entire demeanor registered agitation.

"News from your brother?" Annejoule guessed.

"Yes. The calamity at the oil well is much worse than can be believed. It seems the oil company has been lying to the government and to the public."

"And ...?" Jeanine let the question hang.

"Fedji has colleagues close to the place where this disaster has occurred, aboard research ships. The situation is catastrophic and getting worse each hour. Billions of liters ..."

Annejoule interrupted, "Billions?"

Dan-Dan scratched his chin and seemed to consider whether to divert from his report, then nodded, and answered, "You know one hundred is ten tens." Seeing her affirmative bob he continued, "And one thousand is ..."

"Ten one hundreds," she finished.

"One million is one thousand thousands," he went on, "and one billion is one thousand millions."

"Counting sand by the sea," observed Jeanine. "More than many."

"Yes. A huge number. So billions of liters of oil are pouring into the sea, a river of poison emptying into the ocean, and the river gets larger every hour."

Annejoule thought of pooled oil she'd seen at a machinery repair shop, and tried to imagine a glistening river of the stuff flowing into the nearby bay. As the enormity of the problem overwhelmed her comprehension, she sensed Naoki's voice, in the margins of her thought. *What is it?* he asked. *Oil catastrophe worse than reported-billions of liters spilled,* she replied. *How do you know?* he countered. *Dan-Dan's brother Fedji a chemist in Miami. Who is Dan-Dan? My teacher. How does Fedji know? His colleagues in the Gulf.* All of which seemed to be said in an instant, a flash of intuition. Or imagination? Then, *Is there an attempt to stop this horror?*

She asked aloud, "Is there an attempt to stop this horror?"

Dan-Dan replied, "Fedji tells me the company claims to be working at the problem. But clearly to no avail. Have you learned anything from the dolphins?"

"Silver Singer tells me that others of her kind have begged noisemakers—that is, people—to help. They try to contact people aboard boats, but none seem to understand. Or, they can do nothing. And ..." here she paused.

"Yes, child."

"Many are dying."

"I knew that must be true."

"But good has come of your warning. Many among the dolphins and whales received Silver Singer's message, and swam away. Many have been saved."

"Thank Agwe," intoned Jeanine. At which Dan-Dan and Annejoule exchanged a knowing glance, while the girl felt once again, and sharply, the tension between lost comfort and unbounded freedom in her growing nonbelief..

Who is Agwe? came the voice in Annejoule's head. Who is *Agwe?*

Kushimoto, Japan

Kinyōbi, 29 April, 2010

Amidst the clamor of student voices in the university hallway, it proved difficult to speak loudly enough to be heard, and yet quietly enough to not be overheard. Naoki leaned toward his companion and half-whispered, "The thoughts of this Haitian girl, as with dolphins, I sometimes hear."

"Naokisan, imagination it might be," intoned Takusan, with a deep note of skepicism in his voice. "Proof you have?"

"Data concerning the BP blowout, from this Annejoule I apparently receive."

"All over the news that story ..."

"Her information the Web reports precedes ..."

"Dolphins in the Gulf would know ..."

"Dolphin communication different. Ambiguous. Feeling not facts. Food a constant theme. Sing-song. With ad jingles laced."

"Her source? Haiti from Lousiana distant is."

"Her teacher's brother in the United States apparently a chemist, somehow connected ... yet too, the name Agwe I hear."

"And ...?"

"Googled. A voodoo god."

Takusan laughed, "Scientific that sounds! A journal you are keeping?"

As the friends approached their organic chemistry classroom, Naoki held up his phone. "Here. And in the cloud."

Kushimoto, Japan

Doyōbi, 30 April, 2010

Chicako listened, somewhat impatiently, though not without interest, to her boyfriend's rambling account and musings concerning his apparent telepathic linkage and news of the Deepwater blowout, but finally broke in. "For dolphins in the Gulf nothing here can be done."

"True, but ..."

"Activists in Taiji have organized. Protest planned."

"When?"

"Mokuyōbi. 13 Gogatsu."

"Two weeks off. Exams. Attend I cannot."

"Kaeda and I will go. One day only, off work."

"Safety ...?

"Protest peaceful. Safe enough."

"Numbers?"

"Estimate difficult. Perhaps hundreds. Your knowledge sharing would ..."

Naoki cut in. "Not yet. Soon, perhaps."

"Humanity with compassion begins," Chicako whispered.

Naoki looked down and responded, quietly, with another aphorism, "The tiger its skin saves, a man his reputation."

"Of Basho reminded I am," she answered, taking Naoki's hand.

On a withered bough

A crow alone is perching

Autumn evening now.

He sat silent for several minutes and then wondered aloud, "And Naoki a crow alone?"

Kissing him Chicako responded, "Alone in some ways. In others, than anyone I have ever known more connected. And with you always I am."

Ca Ira, Haiti

Jeudi, 6 May 2010

"Very little is the answer."

Annejoule studied Dan-Dan's face, feeling his frustration at the continuing plight of people in the cities. "You say more than two hundred thousand souls went *anba dlo*—under the water— after the earthquake, and for the survivors?"

"Very little help." Her teacher had returned after several days visiting Port au Prince, where he'd traveled on his motor scooter. The experience had left him deeply dejected. "Tens of thousands living in squalor and mud and sewage. Clean water scarce and not enough food. We will certainly see a cholera epidemic before long. I am heartsick for my country."

"We can help concerning the food," Annejoule insisted.

"Will the dolphins feed a nation?"

"Not that. We can teach people to grow vegetables. Jeanine knows so much, and we can help others to learn."

"Inviting others here, we would soon be overrun."

"But there is unused land between here and town. Do you know the owners of that land?" She gestured at the weed-covered vacant parcels facing Dan-Dan's hut. "Perhaps they would help?"

Dan-Dan brightened, "Perhaps. And if we only invited a few. Young people, like you, eager to learn ... And there is, or was, an agricultural cooperative in Léogâne."

"Jeanine says this planting season continues through May."

"For manioc, yes, this is the time. Too late, I think, for others to start this year. But the need will not fade. The soil is poor, but it can be worked for next season." He nodded toward the nearby fields. "There is much clearing to be done before planting can occur. Jeanine would know better than I what steps to take."

"Will you talk to the owners? Or introduce me? I would ask."

Dan-Dan smiled, "And if you asked, Annejoule, how could they refuse?"

Taiji, Japan

Mokuyōbi. 13 May, 2010

Chicako lofted her sign. "Slaughter must be Stopped!" and looked around at the boisterous crowd. Many dozens of signs, tee shirts and banners reiterated variations of her own message. A young man with a bull horn was leading cacaphonous chants. Television cameras panned the crowd while reporters interviewed protest leaders near the wharf.

"What do we want?"

"Dolphin safety!"

"When do we want it?"

"Now!"

A small group of fishermen stood at one periphery of the milling protesters, shaking their fists and spouting angry commands. "Go away! Troublemakers Taiji leave!"

A clustered group of teens were outfitted in blue sailor-suit uniforms and were wearing cotton medical masks that covered their mouths and noses. Kaeda gestured in their direction. "The hell that is?"

Chicako laughed. "Tokyo many the same do. Disease they fear. Or kissing!" She spotted Shoichi some distance away and tugged on Kaeda's shirt. "This way," she suggested, and began to push through the shouting activists.

"Over two hundred," Kaeda observed. "Possibly three."

As the two women drew near, Chicako shouted, "Shoichi!" and the young man turned his head and smiled in recognition.

"Chicako! Good it is you to see!" He bowed slightly at her approach.

Returning the gesture she replied, "And you!" Then an introduction, "My friend Kaeda this is. From Kushimoto as well."

"National media a pleasant surprise seeing!"

"True," Kaeda agreed. "And perhaps 300 ..."

"More than hoped."

The trio continued conversing, joining in the chanting at times and lofting their signs as photographers circled the crowd. They soon joined in a march from the docks to the town hall where the demonstration concluded with a short speech by one of the organizers.

As the crowd dispersed, they made their way to a small restaurant where the conversation soon veered off into personal stories and discussion of current events.

Relaxed in the company of her best friend and a dedicated ally, Chicako decided to share Naoki's experience. "Knowledge of dolphins I would share," she began. "Secrecy absolute must be."

Her companions understood the serious tone, despite their puzzlement, and quickly assented."

"Again, this urgent is. Secrecy absolute, at least for now."

Both nodded once more.

"With me safe," promised Shoichi.

"Always," added Kaeda.

Looking around to assure herself that no possible listeners were nearby, Chicako quietly recounted Naoki's growing connection with dolphins and Annejoule.

Shoichi spoke first, "Hard is believing."

"Naoki very serious is," Kaeda affirmed. "Not fanciful."

"If true, proof of great intelligence this is !"

"Naoki doubting expects. Presently unwilling public to go," Chicako explained. "Crazy he might seem."

"True enough."

Kaeda inquired, "Considering however?"

"Yes, considering."

Ca Ira, Haiti

Samedi, 15 May, 2010

"Annejoule, meet Webster Moderse."

Annejoule had waded La Rouyonne and joined her
teacher, then walked through weed-covered fields lined with
palms. Dan-Dan had pointed out that even the weeds were faring
poorly due to the spent soil. "Used up," he had observed.

"But improvement is possible," the girl insisted.

Now she spoke to the owner of the land. "Bon apre-midi,
Mesye Moderse." She extended her hand.

Taking hold with both of his, the old man replied,
"Anchante. A friend of Dan-Dan can call me Web."

"Annejoule has an idea, Web. And she needs your help."

With raised eyebrows he responded, "An idea?"

"People are hungry, since ..."

"Ah, yes girl. People are hungry."

"Aid is slow."

"Or nonexistent."

"People can grow food ..."

"But they have forgotten how ..."

"But they can learn. Jeanine is wise in the ways of plants."
This wasn't going exactly as Annejoule had hoped, but Webster
smiled so she plunged ahead. "I want to start a school. For young
women to learn from Jeanine. About planting. About growing."

"And my role?"

"You have this land." She gestured toward the sandy

expanse she and Dan-Dan had just traversed. "Would it be possible?"

"Possible. But land has value. Would you pay rent?"

She laughed, "Web, I haven't a centime. But if the students work the land, build the soil, the land will be improved. It will be better for the use."

"That will require a great deal of work."

"Men anpil, chay pa lou," was her response. "Many hands make the work go swiftly."

"And you promise Web the first melon?"

Annejoule extended her hand again, nodding, "A deal?"

"A deal."

Kushimoto, Japan

Nichiyōbi, 16 May, 2010

"Kaeda I told, and Shoichi."

"What? My secret it was!" Naoki's face registered alarm.

Chicako had reported on the dolphin protest in Taiji as the pair sat on a blanket in their cove, waiting until the last to mention her sharing of Naoki's cetacean communication.

"Trusted they can be."

He closed his eyes, pursed his lips, puffed his cheeks and blew a long sigh. Then rubbing his forehead, "Even monkeys from trees fall."

"Trust me."

"That I do my dearest Chako. And Kaeda. But ..."

Chicako took his hand, "Shoichi, too. On our side he is. A secret deeper his as well."

"Yes?"

"Of young dolphins a release."

"How?

"Clandestine. From cages in the harbor. Scuba. At night. With headlamps. With wire cutters."

"Who?"

"Shoichi. Two others the swim team from."

"When?"

"Soon. Date undetermined."

"Danger."

"Extreme."

Léogâne, Haiti

Mercredi, 19 May, 2010

Poussez was clearly unhappy at being left behind, but Annejoule couldn't see any way to include her on the scooter ride to Léogâne. Jeanine tied a short length of rope around the dog's neck and held her back as the young woman started toward Dan-Dan's home. She could hear the pup whining and barking most of the way to the ford.

Dan-Dan was ready to go when she arrived and they were soon bumping down the dirt track into Ca Ira, and thence bouncing on the rough pavement toward the city. At first the uncertain passenger gripped hands with her arms encircling her teacher, but gradually gained a degree of comfort and shifted to clutching the rim of the seat. The novelty of motor transport and the quickly shifting scenery soon had her grinning and laughing.

The goal today was recruitment, starting with a search for Ghislaine. With Dan-Dan's protection and his comfort with the authorities, Annejoule was optimistic that they would be able to track down her best friend and through her some other young women who might be interested in what she now called the École des Dauphins. Dan-Dan had contacted the Agricultural Cooperative as well, though news on that front was not good. It seemed to have fallen into complete disarray after the earthquake, with the organizers, like everyone else, coping with simple survival. But the contact might lead to a source for seeds.

Dan-Dan stopped to inquire of a friend working with

Medecins Sans Frontieres, who looked through a database of patients treated since the quake. Ghislaine Laurence had sought treatment for cuts and bruising a month past. Her father, Phillipe, had listed their address as Chatulet Road and Rue de Sacre Coeur.

The ride to that intersection wasn't long at all, but the sight that greeted them on arrival was grim. A vast expanse of tarps and tents stretched out over what might have once been farm land. Dan-Dan parked and locked his scooter, then they set out on foot to make inquiries among the refugees in the camp.

Almost an hour went by before a woman brightened and nodded, "Yes. Phillipe Laurence. Just down the way. With his family." And minutes later Annejoule was embracing her friend.

"Annejoule, I was so worried for you. Your whole apartment block ..."

"Maman and Justy ..." she looked down, her expression saying all that could be said.

"Oh, amou kè, I am so sorry ..."

"So many have lost so much. And you Ghislaine? The doctors treated you?"

Her friend's voice dropped to a near whisper. "Raped. Like so many. By more than one."

The young women embraced again, both sobbing, for loss and for finding the other alive. For all the ways their world had changed, and for the constancy of friendship through the time of suffering. Ghislaine explained that the family's landlord had evicted them, hence their presence in the camp, and she had some news of others among their friends, several who had survived and some who had died in the quake.

"Marie?"

"Non." sighed Ghislaine. "L'al bwachat. And her whole family."

Annejoule gripped her friend's hands, all the sorrowful losses welling up, each compounding the others. Was there no end to the pain?

Finally shaking off the dire news, Annejoule shifted the conversation to her farm school. Would Ghislaine want to join her? Without question. Would she help recruit others? Of course. Could she plan to come to Ca Ira by mid-June?

"I could join you today," was the instant answer.

"I'll need you to talk to others here, first."

"Of course. But soon?"

"Yes soon." Annejoule pulled Dan-Dan away from his conversation with Phillipe, and with his assurance told her friend, "Dan-Dan will come for you in two weeks."

The girls embraced again, each bolstered by the small step back toward normalcy in the midst of catastrophic change.

Kushimoto, Japan

Kayōbi, 1 June, 2010

"Annejoule a farm school is organizing."

Takusan stifled a yawn and didn't sound much interested when he replied, "Yes?"

"Haitian hunger widespread to the earthquate consequent."

"And?"

"I wish to help," Naoki answered.

"You a farmer?" Takusan laughed aloud. "When since? A bluefin farmer, yes. But plants?"

"Crowdfunding. Money raised can be. Your assistance most valuable that regard within." Naoki knew that his friend had garnered thousands of yen for his amateur baseball club via the Web. "For your Dodgers you raised ... how much?"

"True. A lot."

"And your expertise available now is?"

"Could I refuse? But to this Haitian woman funds can travel?"

Naoki grinned. "Covered. Fedji a chemist in Miami is."

"So?"

"Google. Fedji. Miami. Chemistry. Only one University of Miami chemistry professor named Fedji exists. Fedji Wilsen Dieujuste. E-mails exchanged. Funds to Dan-Dan he will convey."

"Dan-Dan? Reminder needed."

"Annejoule's teacher."

Ca Ira, Haiti

Mercredi, 2 June, 2010

When Dan-Dan returned from the city with Ghislaine aboard his scooter, Annjoule was waiting on his porch. As her friend dismounted, she ran over and embraced her, laughing.

"At last!"

"That was some ride!"

"Thanks Dan-Dan. You're the best!"

Soon the girls were caught up in conversation about plans for the school. "Daphcar and her sister Lucsenda, Perpétue, you remember, her mother has one arm? Anieltha, who I met in the camp. Saraphina and Modelaine, who I know from church. All of them want to join. They'll all travel together on July 1."

Annejoule counted on her fingers. "So we'll start with eight. That's wonderful!"

"They should be safe in a group."

"We'll go get them, to show the way."

"Where is the farm?"

Annejoule pointed, proudly, at the dusty field on the opposite side of the road. "There."

"It doesn't look like much. The weeds aren't even ..."

"It will change. We will change it."

"Are you sure?"

"Jeanine will show us how. And now, grab your backpack, and come meet her."

As they passed through Jeanine's garden, Ghislaine's

doubts faded somewhat. "This is so beautiful!"

"And we can do the same."

Soon introductions were made, and Laban seemed happier than he'd been in some time, seeing a familar face from his birthplace.

Ca Ira, Haiti
Jeudi, 3 June, 2010

The two friends had talked far into the night and so rose late. Jeanine was already busy in the garden, but had set out a special breakfast for them. They ate quickly, then went to join their mentor.

"Dan-Dan said we'll need fertilizer," Annejoule offered.

"Fertilizer is expensive."

"Dan-Dan says some farmers use fish scraps."

"Even those have a price, my daughter. When my Louis was here ..." she sighed.

"What Jeanine?"

"My compost was so rich."

"Louis, you've told me, was a great fisherman. I wish we knew another ..." Annejoule scratched her head.

"There are far fewer fish today, in the bay. Louis' youngest brother Mackenly still goes out in some seasons. He says there are fewer and fewer snapper, and more and more jellyfish. Moon jellies, he calls them, and they are beyond numbering in the summer."

"Wouldn't they make good fertilizer, too?" Ghislaine asked. "In school we learned that decaying animal bodies release nitrogen."

"I suppose they would," Jeanine nodded. Then, having thought it through for a few moments, "Yes."

Annejoule mused aloud, "If only we had a boat and a net."

"Mackenly still has Louis' boat."

Ghislaine asked the obvious next question. "Can we use it? "Do you know how?"

"We can learn," Annejoule insisted. "And we will."

Kushimoto, Japan

Mokuyōbi, 17 June, 2010

¥46,897!

YIKES!

:D

U SUMTH R!

MNY HLP

U IT DID!

Naoki texted Chicako during class, after Takusan texted the latest fundraising results. Donations had come in from all around the world, it seemed, small amounts here and there, though most were from fellow students or research fellows at Kinki University. Later the trio met at Naoki's apartment.

"¥47,000 in Haiti amounts to?"

"22,000 gourdes approximately." Naoki reported. "Online currency converter indicates."

Chicako bit her lip, then asked,"Which buys?"

"Minimum wage 200 gourdes per day."

Chicako did some quick calculations on her phone. "For a full day, half of our minimum wage per hour they receive."

"And unemployment fifty percent or more maintaining."

"Poverty astonishing," added Takusan.

"Poorest nation the Americas within," added Naoki. "And so this charity therefore to more than 100 days pay amounts. Not inconsiderable."

"True that." said his girlfriend, smiling. "True that."

Ca Ira, Haiti

Dimanche, 20 June, 2010

"What are we going to do with them if we get any?" Ghislaine's stubborn practicality was all too present as Annejoule pulled on the heavy wooden oars.

"We'll figure something out," was her only response.

Having recovered the fishing boat from Mackenly, together with some words of advice, the two young women had headed out into the bay to practice rowing just two days after they'd learned of the boat's existence. On ensuing days they'd alternated their nautical practice with mending of an old baitfish seine Mackenly had likewise provided.

Jeanine's experience with nets had, as with gardening, proved invaluable. They had quickly patched gaps in the net and then benefited equally from the elder woman's knowledge of how to play out and then gather up the fishing gear.

Today was their first attempt to put the boat and net and advice into practice.

Still reluctant to share her experience of dolphin communication beyond Jeanine and Dan-Dan, Annejoule hadn't told her friend that the jellyfishing expedition was being guided by Silver Singer.

Ghislaine had been impatient when Annejoule insisted on rowing a kilometer or more from their launch point. "Why not try here?" she'd queried. "There must be jellyfish all over the bay."

"There are a lot more off the point," Annjoule had

declared.

"How do you know?"

"I know," she'd rejoined.Then, "Look! Dolphins!"

Not far from the boat, the pod was cruising along, keeping pace with their rowing.

Once Silver Singer had assured Annejoule that she was in the thick of the current jellyfish invasion, she told Ghislaine that it was time to spread the net. Leaving one end attached to a plastic-bottle buoy, they fed out the seine in a wide arc. Next the two rowed together, each on one oar, pulling hard as they brought the ends of the net together, and then proceeded to tow it toward shore, with the dolphins following behind.

"Amazing," muttered Ghislaine, though it wasn't clear whether she was commenting on the marine mammals or their catch. The seine was packed with quivering blobs of jellyfish.

With all of their strength the young women pulled the seine shoreward. As they dragged it up toward the beach it was apparent that it contained hundreds of kilos of gelatinous matter. With each advancing wave they tugged it further up the strand. At the end of their strength they had managed to pull the quivering mound just above the high tide line.

"Now what?" Ghislaine asked aloud.

"We'll figure something out," Annejoule answered, breathing hard.

Amidst the gelatinous mound, a good number of silvery baitfish wiggled and squirmed. Annejoule plucked some of them from the pile and tossed them toward the dolphins, still swimming close to the shore. Silver Singer and others bobbed up and caught the fish as they landed.

"Fish, fish, fish, fish, fish!" Annejoule heard their thoughts. And "Thank you noisemaker friend."

Ghislaine joined in the picking and tossing, and both women laughed aloud at the acrobatics of the spinners.

Then they pulled the boat up onto the beach, well above the tideline, turned it over, and stashed the oars underneath.

As they picked their way back toward home, Ghislaine pointed out the too obvious facts.

"We're going to need a way to move that mountain of jellyfish to the garden."

"I know."

"How?"

"We'll figure it out."

"How did you know where all those jellyfish were swimming?"

"I'll tell you soon."

"Where are our friends going to sleep?"

"In tents."

"What tents?"

"We'll figure that out. Or maybe under the boat. Or in trees like monkeys. Somewhere."

"You are a completely crazy optimist." Ghislaine shook her head. "I love you, but you are crazy."

"Probably. But who found the jellyfish?"

Ca Ira, Haiti

Lundi, 21 June, 2010

"Do you know someone named Matsumoto Naoki?" Dan-Dan had appeared at Jeanine's late on Monday morning.

Annejoule was startled. "Naoki?"

"Yes, Matsumoto Naoki."

With Ghislaine beside her, as yet uninformed about the strange dolphin communication, Annejoule was reluctant to admit too much. "The name is strange, but not unfamiliar." She winked at Dan-Dan, hoping he wouldn't press the question. "Why do you ask?"

"This Matsumoto has sent you money, via my brother Fedji, for your school."

"What? Money? For the school? What does that mean?"

Dan-Dan smiled, "This Matsumoto has sent a check for 22,000 gourdes to help with the project."

Annejoule reeled. The amount was more money than she had ever imagined having at one time in her life.

"And we can use it for the school?" she asked, not entirely sure of what it meant to 'get a check' or how they would possibly spend such riches.

"Of course."

"We need a hand cart or a wheelbarrow and shovels and four tents and we need food," she spurted. "The other six will join us in ten days."

"The tools are not a problem. The food we'd best discuss with Jeanine."

Soon Dan-Dan was on his way to purchase the requisite supplies while Ghislaine was full of questions.

"Matsumoto sounds like a Japanese name."

"Yes."

"So you know someone in Japan?"

"Sort of."

"In Japan?"

"Well, I know his name."

"You know his name and he's sending you a fortune?"

"Um ..."

"A boyfriend? You've got a rich boyfriend?"

"It's not like that."

"What's it like?"

Annejoule sighed and sat down where she stood. "Can you keep a secret? I mean, I know you can keep a secret. What I mean is, will you? A big secret?"

Ghislaine settled beside her. "You're my best friend, Ahnie."

With that the young woman began to tell the story of the voices, the dolphins, and her growing connection to the unseen Naoki half a world away. "And that's how I knew where the jellyfish were concentrated," she finished.

"From Naoki?" Ghislaine sounded completely at sea.

"No, from Silver Singer."

"But Naoki knew about our farm school?"

"From me, I guess. Or the dolphins."

Ghislaine considered the answer for several minutes, picking up a stick and sketching randomly in the dirt, then blurted, "How does he understand you?"

"I don't know."

"I mean, in Japan they speak Japanese, and here we speak French, or something like French. Creole they call our speech. How does he understand you?"

"Or I him ..." Annejoule added. "I don't know. Perhaps we should ask Dan-Dan."

Kushimoto, Japan

Kayōbi, 22 June, 2010

Naoki dug a wide-bladed shovel into mounded chopped mackerel in a wheelbarrow and flung the contents into swirling green water which immediately exploded into foam. Young bluefins devoured their food faster than he could heave it into their midst, upper fins creasing the water as they raced back and forth in the massive holding pen.

In a few minutes Takusan arrived, pushing a second barrowful of feed down the narrow floating dock. "This one I'll empty," he offered, noting the glaze of sweat on his friend's face. "Sometimes more slavery than education to me this seems."

Naoki nodded. "But exercise the mind clears, or so Koichi insists."

"And when it is the mackerel he hauls and shovels?"

"Other days," Naoki shrugged. "Not ours to question, really."

"True enough. The check you sent? And received?"

"Fedji confirmed. Brother Dan-Dan Annejoule's elation. You my friend the only funding source provided."

"Your idea, Naokisan. To you the credit due." Takusan took the shovel and began to offload fish as speeding tuna continued to roil the water. "News of Shoichi's plan?"

Naoki looked around before answering in a lowered voice. "Chicako delay in plan reports. Until Kugatsu, time of next capture."

"And slaughter," returned his friend.

A pod of dolphins swam into view out beyond the nets.

"Waveweaver among them," said Naoki.

"What saying?"

"I think they understand what we're doing here. 'Fish, fish, fish, fish, fish,' she's singing, along with the rest, and laughing. Sometimes conversations we have, and sometimes just carefree they seem. Every ad jingle ever written they apparently remember. Now a Coke they'd like the world to buy."

"Aquatic cola wars ensuing?"

"Could be."

But Naoki heard much more than he could readily relate to his friend. The dolphin's singing had become a quiet soundtrack in his mind, like elevator music or SiriusXM in a dental office. The squeaks and grunts and squeals seemed to recede, while the apparently ancient tales of their cetacean kin intruded. The stories were more felt than understood verbatim, and he couldn't have clearly articulated their content had he tried. A deep sense of the joy of freedom, the pleasure of affinity, a confidence in the continuity of life, and the powerful sensation of swimming often came upon him unbidden.

We sing, we sing, we sing the silver sea.

We swim, we swim, we swim the wild waves.

Squidapple, squideemish, squididly, squidance.

Sun kissed skin, so hot, will melt your popsicle.

We sing the silver sea.

"And pop songs," Naoki added. "Every last one they know."

Ca Ira, Haiti

Mardi, 22 June, 2010

The two friends were up early, eager to see the results of Dan-Dan's shopping expedition. He had borrowed Web's ancient pick-up truck and returned from Léogâne with more tools than Annejoule had thought to order. Shovels, rakes, hoes, a pitchfork, a big-wheeled hand cart, a wheelbarrow and four sturdy tents, several buckets (some with lids), a few tarps and meters of rope. Many of the items were used, but all serviceable. Joyous tears rolled down her face as she examined the lot, the École des Dauphins seeming all the more real.

Holding up the largest shovel she asked, "This is a strange shovel. Too large and square to push into the ground, I think. What is it for, Dan-Dan?"

"It's called a manure shovel. Usually used to clean out animal pens, horses, goats ..."

"We haven't anything but Jeanine's few chickens."

Dan-Dan smiled broadly and laughed. "Annjoule, you have a huge pile of stinking jellyfish."

As they carried the gear to the thinly wooded lot they'd chosen for a camp site, Ghislaine posed her language question. "Annejoule told me about the dolphins, and her communication with Naoki. How do you think it possible that they can understand each other, speaking different languages?"

"That has puzzled me too, Ghislaine. And to tell the truth, while I love our Ahnie, and completely believed her concerning the dolphins, I wasn't entirely sure about this Naoki ..."

"You didn't believe me?" Annejoule exclaimed.

"Not that, exactly, but you are dealing with something entirely new to me. I'd guess it is entirely new to all of humanity. Certainly that's what the dolphins have told you. And human imagination is powerful. Remember our discussion of gods?"

"That's so," she assented. "And how could you be sure I wasn't ..."

"Exactly. But now this money, from Naoki, to Fedji, to me, to you. That tells me that, whatever the connection you might have with this man in Japan, he certainly learned my name, my brother's name, his location in the United States, and, of course, your plans for a farm school."

Ever the sleuth, Ghislaine asked, "How could he find your brother?"

Dan-Dan made the best explanation he could of the internet, computers, search engines, and other bits of the global communication system, so remote from the experience of young Haitian women.

The women nodded, shot each other wide-eyed looks, and giggled. Finally Annejoule said, "I hear you, but, absent these tools and tents, I would easily think it was all in your imagination!"

Ghislaine returned to her original question. "But how does Ahnie understand this Naoki? If the dolphins carry her messages in Creole, and repeat them as they do our advertising songs, how would he comprehend. Or the same in reverse?"

"Ah, yes. I am not an expert, having been a professor of history, not language. But over the years I read a bit, and attended some lectures by those who study such things. Linguists they are called, because they study language."

They had reached the camp and Annjoule suggested raking out tent sites. As they cleared and leveled the sandy soil, Dan-Dan continued.

"Linguists believe that every human being has an innate language ability. Something we are born with. Something in our brains that allows us to learn language and arrange words into sentences."

"Laban is always surprising me," Annjoule observed. "He overhears our adult conversations and makes up complicated stories."

"Just so," the teacher agreed. "And now, it would seem, Ahnie has discovered that the dolphins share this ability."

"Only, without sound," Ghislaine added.

"Ah, that is called telepathy, and is another piece of the puzzle entirely. But let's stay with the language for now. You both have enough school experience to have learned about nouns, verbs, adjectives and so forth?"

"Yes, years ago!"

"Well, in our language, we make sentences with a subject, and a verb. 'Birds fly,' for instance."

"Poussez runs," said Annejoule.

"Poussez runs fast!" added her friend.

"Exactly, and so we build sentences out of all of those names and actions and other words that modify them. Those parts of speech occur in every language on earth. But people use very different words to fill in. We say 'dauphin,' the English say 'dolphin,' and the Japanese use a word that I can't even pronounce. But it means the same."

"Why are there so many languages?" Ghislaine prodded.

"Now you are talking history, about which I know much more. After humans evolved from apes, we began to speak. Or, perhaps that's when we stopped being apes."

"The preacher man said that evolution is a lie and speaking of it is a sin."

"Then, I think, this is going to be a very, very long conversation," Dan-Dan sighed.

Kushimoto, Japan

Nichiyōbi, 27 June, 2010

Chicako stretched out on the blanket and yawned. "So good the sun feels." The pair were savoring a visit to their cove, had swum and picnicked and finally, simply, relaxed, listening to the sussing of waves and the laughing cries from a flock of black-tailed gulls overhead.

"Nesting they are," said Naoki, gesturing at the milling birds. He leaned back and pointed upward, "The cliffs upon."

"Lucky birds."

"Such luck you should have?"

"Nesting, yes."

"Next spring." He reached to pull her into an embrace.

Chicako pulled closer and stuck her tongue in his ear, then whispered, "Proposing you are?"

"That I had already done, I thought."

"Actually, no."

"Then, yes."

She rolled away, "Indefinite sounding."

"You me will marry?" he asked. "Naokisan the happiest human on our small planet making?"

Chicako mocked indecision, sat up, tapped her index finger on her chin and raised it as if to make a point, then drilled it into Naoki's chest. "You I love! Most emphatically, yes!"

"Accountability urgent," he replied, pretending a sterness he obviously did not feel. "No sooner than graduation in March, no later than June? Uncertainty now absent?"

Rolling atop him and laughing, she replied, "Terms acceptable. You passionate, idiotic nerd! Second happiest human instantly you have become."

Ca Ira, Haiti

Jeudi, 1 July, 2010

Annejoule and Ghislaine had left the school camp at daybreak and walked toward Léogâne on the Route de Ca Ira. Poussez bounded ahead or veered off into the underbrush beside patches of farm land, but stayed nearby where houses were close together, barking now and again at other dogs.

Half-way to the city, they saw a cluster of young women approaching, who proved to be their expected students. Excited reunion and introductions ensued, including a new recruit.

"This is my dear friend Marie," Perpétue offered, "I hoped it would be alright if ..."

"Of course," Annejoule interrupted. "I am so glad that all of you could join the Ecole des Dauphins, and I hope we can invite many more in the future. Hunger might as well be our nation's name."

Anieltha looked around at her companions. "We've all lost weight," she observed.

"And friends," added Saraphina.

"And families," Annjoule looked down, suddenly choked with loss. Ghislaine hugged her and pulled her head to her shoulder.

"So much loss."

As they headed back to the school camp, the mood lightened, and Annjoule explained her ideas for the farm school. "It will mean a lot of hard work, but Jeanine is so wise, we will all be learning a lot about feeding ourselves and our families. And

Dan-Dan wants to teach us history and other subjects ... that is, anyone who wants to continue with regular schooling. It's up to you. And don't think that I believe I have all the answers. We will all make this happen, and everyone's ideas will be welcome."

"Why do you call it Ecole des Dauphins," asked Daphcar.

"A long story, that. Which I'll share in due time."

Annejoule exchanged glances with Ghislaine. "Let's just say, for now, that I greatly admire the beautiful dolphins in the bay. You will too, when you see them."

"And it needed a name," added Ghislaine.

Soon enough they arrived at the camp, sorted out sleeping arrangements and stowed their small bundles of clothing. It was clear that three would be a crowd in the wall tents they'd procured, so Annejoule announced she'd return to Jeanine's. "I need to care for Laban, so that's probably best anyway," she offered.

"Can we start right away?" asked Modelaine. "I've been twitching to get started ever since Ghislaine told me about this plan. And life in the refugee camp was so incredibly boring!"

Annejoule laughed. "How do you feel about shoveling jellyfish?"

Soon Ghislaine led the newcomers to the shore, towing the hand cart. Some set to work shoveling the stinky dead mass into the cart while others collected driftwood.

Annejoule returned to Jeanine's to inform her of the arrival and then went to her listening station on the beach, carrying a bucket.

"Silver Singer, my friends have come to learn to grow food. Can I ask a favor?"

"We sing, we sing, we sing our friendship."

"Can you bring me fish, more than usual?"

"You give us fish. We give you fish. Sweet dreams are made of these, who am I to disagree? Fish, fish, fish, fish, fish."

Soon fins appeared in the bay and a large pod of dolphins headed toward shore to release fresh caught snapper. Annejoule counted as she put them in her bucket. Ten.

"Oh, thankyou Silver Singer. Thank you all!"

That evening the schoolmates enjoyed a celebratory feast, with Dan-Dan, Jeanine and Laban joining in.

Ca Ira, Haiti

Samedi, 10 July, 2010

"Heisenberg!" Annejoule jolted awake, aware that the strange word she had heard came from her own mouth. What did it mean?

She immediately remembered a very vivid, explicitly erotic dream. Her breathing was shallow and fast. She wiped beads of persperation from her forehead as she tried to remember. That it had been of a couple making love she was sure, but it seemed somehow that she had been the man involved. She had looked down at a slender woman's body moving beneath her, a body so very different from her own. The skin color recalled beach sand or weather-burnished welk shells she'd picked up on the strand. The face. Mouth slightly open, rounded as if saying "oh." Closed eyes then opening wide, the "oh" stretching into a smile, then laughing. The face framed with straight black hair. All half-recollected and now quickly fading, all but that strange word and a memory of deeply pleasurable motion.

Was that how some experienced sex? That would be so wonderful.

Then her thoughts flashed back to her would-be rapists in Léogâne. Would she ever be able to trust a man to be with her that way? Her thoughts turned to Dan-Dan. So it wasn't all men who were bad. Surely Dan-Dan had been as kind and thoughtful when he was her age. And the man in her dream. Surely he loved that pale-skinned woman.

And then aloud, "Naoki. Was that Naoki?"

Jeanine heard her and called out softly, "Everything alright?"

"Yes, mon Maman, it was just a dream."

Kushimoto, Japan

Doyōbi, 10 July, 2010

Chicako snuggled closer to Naoki and interlaced her fingers with his. The lovers had spent the afternoon in his apartment, with the music videos on Naoki's TV turned down low.

Her phone beeped, and she plucked it from the floor.

PLNS SET read the text message.

"Shoichi," she explained, pointing at the screen. "Two months from today the message means."

"Dolphin drive begins when?"

"30 Hachigatsu. Early this year. Reason unknown."

"Who Shoichi's plan knows?"

"The three in Taiji, you and I, and Kaeda and Takusan. As far aware as I am. Training constantly."

"At night the release?"

"Harbor in daylight too busy."

"Brave men."

"True that," Chicako replied. She clicked to a Web site. "Online this poem I found. Sylvie Prouvaire the author."

"French the name sounds."

The valiant dreamer

Composes rhymes, watches clouds

And weeps over love.

"Shoichi a valiant dreamer?"

"And Naoki," Chicako answered, embracing him once more.

Ca Ira, Haiti

Mercredi, 21 July, 2010

In the first three weeks the students of the Ecole des Dauphins had organized their camp site, dragged up a weathered table found amidst the flotsam on the shore, fashioned a bathing stall with one tarp and a toilet stall with another.

Dan-Dan had explained the idea of a composting toilet arrangement that he'd learned from a nonprofit charity in Port au Prince. "You use the bucket, and throw in sawdust or dirt after each use, and close the lid tight to keep out flies. When the bucket is full, you add it to a hot compost. That kills insect eggs and disease germs."

"How do we make it hot?" asked Ghislaine.

"By layering plant material, with your manure and dirt. As with other animals, our waste contains nitrogen and minerals from the food we eat. Your hair contains nitrogen, so when you clean a hairbrush you can add that. And your jellyfish are another nitrogen source."

Annejoule interjected, "That's what Jeanine does, though she describes it differently."

Daphcar laughed. "I'm not an animal!"

Her sister poked her arm, "Sometimes I'm not sure."

"It seems kind of yucky to me." Perpétue stuck out her tongue. "Yeck."

Dan-Dan grinned, "Well, we are part of the natural world. Plants feed animals and animals feed plants. Round and round.

When you think of it that way, it's not really yucky, it's seeing that we are all linked to the rest of life here."

"And around the world," added Annejoule. "All around the world."

The first pile of jellyfish had been shoveled into the cart and into trenches in the farm field, together with dried seaweed, and Ghislaine and Annejoule had gone out again for more. This time they had help dragging the heavy net onshore, with an even bigger catch. Once again Annjoule picked out bait fish and tossed them to the dolphins which had followed the net toward shore. Soon all the other women joined in, laughing and applauding the mammal's antics.

"How'd you know where to find them?" Saraphina asked.

"Annejoule has a nose for them," replied Ghislaine.

"The first pile really stank."

"That was because we had collected them awhile before you arrived, and before we had the cart. We'll deal with these quicker."

Once a week they shared a fish feast supplied by Silver Singer and other dolphins, and following the third such meal, Anieltha said she wanted to join Annejoue on her fishing trips. "I used to fish with my father," she explained, "I'm pretty good at it, but not as good as you. Eske ou janm gen devenn?" E

Annejoule and Ghislaine shared knowing glances, their eyes catching glints of firelight. The latter woman tightened her mouth and shrugged, Annejoule sighed and nodded.

"Anieltha, it isn't a matter of luck. Or, at least, it isn't a matter of luck at fishing. I think it's time to tell you all a very big secret," she started.

Lucsenda laughed, "About your anmore?"

"What?"

"Your boyfriend who sent money for tools?"

Annejoule aimed a sharp look at Ghislaine who swallowed hard and said, "Well, they wanted to know how you could buy the tools, and I needed to answer and I sort of told the truth. Perhaps now ... ?"

"Okay. This has got to be a secret. I need to trust all of you to keep it. I really think it would not be good for me, for us, for the school, if this gets out. Can I trust you?"

She looked from woman to woman around the circle, and each in turn nodded. "Of course. Yes. I promise," the affirmations went round.

Annejoule continued. "Okay. After the earthquake, when I was unconscious under the rubble, I began to hear the thoughts of dolphins."

"What?"

"Hearing thoughts?"

"How is that possible?"

"I don't know. But they became clearer and clearer. Just like talking. Only their talk is different. Singing really. Silver Singer is the name of the one with whom I am most in touch."

"That's amazing! You should tell the world! You'd be famous, Ahnie!" Modelaine exclaimed. "Really, you'd be on television."

"And I'd be called a witch. And people would overrun our school. And it would be horrible."

"Of course, that's why the school's name."

"And the fish?" Modelaine asked.

"Yes they bring me fish."

"And your anmore?" Lucsenda giggled. "Is he a dolphin too? Where does a dolphin get money?"

"There's more to the secret. Let me continue. A man named Naoki seems to have had the same experience, in Japan, on the other side of the world."

Lucsenda jumped in, "A Japanese anmore? Amazing!"

"Not a boyfriend. But he learned about this school from the dolphins. He wanted to help, and he raised money in Japan, and sent it to Dan-Dan's brother in Miami, Florida. And Fedji sent it to Dan-Dan, and here we are."

"Can we meet them? I mean, we saw them today, but ..."

Annejoule thought a moment. "I don't see why not."

"Aha!" exclaimed Saraphina, "That's how you find the jellyfish!"

Ca Ira, Haiti

Jeudi, 22 July, 2010

The nine students and Laban hiked to Annejoule's lookout early the next morning. En route she had called out to Silver Singer who answered immediately.

"We sing, we sing, we sing your name! Annejoule my friend, hello. We swim, we swim, we swim. Fish, fish, fish, fish, fish."

"I want my friends to meet you. Are you willing?" she asked, unsure if strangers would in fact be welcome.

"Squidapple, squideemish, Squididdle. We spin, we swim, we sing, we dream. Of course, Annejoule. Of course."

When they reached the shore dolphins were already coming their way, frisking and spinning above the waves. Annejoule shed her clothing, undressed Laban, and walked into the waves holding his hand. The others, with varying degrees of reluctance, gradually followed suit. Soon they were standing neck-deep in the warm bay, and the pod of dolphins were swimming among them.

Gasping with delight, Anieltha stroked one of the large animals saying, "It's true. I wasn't sure I could believe you, but it's true. It's amazing!"

Silver Singer stayed close to Annejoule and Laban, swirling around her, and brushing them gently with her flukes. Then she slid past Lucsenda, and Annejoule heard her thoughts, "A baby, a baby, a baby. We sing, we sing."

Puzzled Annejoule queried, "A baby? Laban?"

"No. A baby, a baby, a baby," came a chorus of dolphin voices as they started back out to sea.

The young women watched the pod until it was out of sight and then walked back to their clothing on the beach. Annejoule noticed Lucsenda's swelling stomach, looked her questioningly in the eye, and looked back down.

Lucsenda nodded.

"Silver Singer told me," Annejoule whispered, quietly enough that none of the others heard. "When due?"

"Five months. Four months."

"Oh, my. Oh, my. And you'll share the news?"

"Now, I suppose. It's not like I'll be hiding it," she whispered in turn.

As they donned their clothing, Lucsenda said aloud, "It's time to share my secret." She pulled up her shirt and patted her belly.

"A baby!" shouted Daphcar.

"Who's?" queried Ghislaine.

"Remember Stanley, at the camp?"

"Handsome boy!" Ghislaine replied.

Perpétue grinned. "I thought you had something going with him. I guess you had a lot going on." She swayed her hips suggestively.

"Does he know?" Ghislaine wondered aloud.

"Not yet."

Daphcar demanded, "Does he love you?"

"Yes."

"Then it should all be okay."

"Annejoule, it would be nice if we had some men in the school."

She patted Lucsenda's stomach, gently, and replied, "It could make things very complicated."

The walk back to the farm was accompanied by noisy chatter about the baby, the dolphins and the boys they'd known at home.

Annejoule was quiet, however. The news and the talk had reminded her of her dreams.

Kushimoto, Japan

Mokuyōbi , 29 July, 2010

"So, a modern wedding then?" Kaeda prodded her friend. "Surely, for my Chako not traditional."

"Modern. A no host party, so the venue we can afford. Hotel banquet room with cash bar might be free."

"Big?"

"Not very. My friends. Naoki's friends. His parents and some cousins. My sister and her husband."

"From Morioka?" Kaeda sipped her tea, and gazed at her best friend across the cafe table.

Chicako nodded. "You I told Kotone pregnant?"

"No! How cool! When due?

"Early Sangatsu, or late Nigatsu. To Morioka then I'll go."

"And a month later, Kotone here for wedding?"

"The plan that is."

"With you there I'd go, if welcome."

"Could do."

"So, the wedding where is?"

"No thought at present. Long time spring remains."

"Never before a wedding have I planned."

"Kaeda! You my wedding planning? News to me."

"Someone must. The photographer is ...?"

"What photographer?" Chicako's brow furrowed.

"A photographer you must have. And a hairdresser. And the gown. Shopping for gown in Wakayama?"

"Kaeda, sumimasen, please calm down!"

"Me you need," her friend replied. "And what's the point of estimating the skin of live tanuki?"

"To what on earth germane that is?"

"No clue. But live tanukis I've always favored."

"You, my friend, beyond belief silly are."

"You, my dearest friend, too serious remain."

Ca Ira, Haiti

Vendredi, 30 July, 2010

At the end of a lesson about Haiti's most recent political upheaval, Saraphina shifted subjects. "Dan-Dan, can you explain how it is that Annejoule understands the dolphins? I keep thinking about it, and I can't figure it out."

"It is very strange, isn't it? There are the two parts. First, the connection is telepathic, that means there is some kind of signal between their brains and hers."

"And Naoki's," added Anieltha.

"Right. And I can't begin to explain that, though there have always been people who claimed they could hear others' thoughts, and some scientists have spent years trying to prove or disprove it. But there are always new discoveries. At one time no one knew of radio waves, but now radios are common."

Lucsenda blurted, "I wish we had one! I miss the music in the city."

"Me too," Ghislaine agreed.

"As for the language," Dan-Dan continued, "That's a little easier to guess. Dolphins are mammals like us. They give birth to live babies and have milk glands to feed the newborns. They breathe air and they communicate with each other with sound."

"But they don't have fingers and toes! Or arms and legs, for that matter," Sarphina observed.

"They used to," Dan-Dan stated flatly, looking around at the students to gauge the reaction. Some of the women frowned and looked doubtful, others less so, and Anieltha was nodding in agreement.

"They went back to the ocean and grew fins!" she added.

"Something like that." Dan-Dan stood. "Wait, I'll get a picture." He went into his house and returned to the porch with a dusty old dictionary. He thumbed through, and found what he was looking for. "See, this is a hippopotamus." He passed the book around so they could all see the line drawing of the beast accompanying the definition and description.

"I don't see any fingers," Saraphina announced.

"Not fingers, but toes. That isn't a very detailed picture. Anyway, the hippopotamus lives in Africa, across the Atlantic Ocean from here. It's a very large, very fat creature that spends most of its time in rivers and a great deal of time under water with only its nostrils above the surface."

"Scientists who study the history of life have studied old bones, bones so old they have turned into rock—called fossils— and they say that animals related to today's hippopotamus became more and more aquatic, 50 or 60 million years ago. Over those millions of years, small changes kept occuring and they gradually became the whales and dolphins in our ocean today."

Saraphina rejected the explanation outright. "That sounds crazy."

"Yes. It does." Dan-Dan agreed. "But it is apparently true. Because other scientist who study living bodies, have discovered something in our cells, in all living cells that make up all living things, that tells a cell how to grow. They call it DNA, which is a short form of a very complicated name, deoxyribonucleic acid.

And they can tell from the DNA of today's hippopotamus and today's whales, that they are relatives, or they were, a long, long time ago."

"I don't get it." Lucsenda shook her head. "How can there be something inside of a body that tells it how to grow?"

"How can there not be?" Ghislaine countered. "Boys look like their fathers, girls look like their mothers, dogs have puppies, mice have whatever you call a baby mouse. Something must tell them how to grow."

Annejoule added, "And that change from hippopotamus to whale is what they call evolution, right?"

Dan-Dan nodded. "And to take it further, it seems that dolphin brains evolved to be very much like our own. Again, other scientists who study brains have shown that the brain of a spinner dolphin, like Silver Singer, is about the same size as a human brain, and is about as complicated as a human brain. Then going a step still further, another kind of scientist, called linguists because they study language, have shown that whales and dolphins definitely communicate with each other, using songs and whistles and clicks. But the scientists don't understand what they are saying to each other."

"Until now," Saraphina affirmed. "I'm not sure I believe the whole story you have told us, but Annejoule is definitely in contact with them."

"And with her anmore," giggled Anieltha.

Kushimoto, Japan

Kayōbi , 4 August, 2010

Takusan and Naoki peered through a glass-bottomed viewer, snapping photos with their cells, in an attempt to estimate the number of bluefin through extrapolation. Repeated instantaneous counts within the viewing field could be used to arrive at an accurate calculation, or so their professor insisted.

"How many shots needed?"

"Fifty, minimum," Naoki replied.

"Average then and multiply by?"

"Area and depth. Schooling uniform shallow to deep?"

Dolphins surfaced just past the end of the dock, exhaling in spurts of spray.

"Knowing how? Shoichi we should call. His scuba to employ." Takusan nodded toward the pod, "Or ask Waveweaver."

Naoki looked around nervously, to assure himself that they were still alone on the docks. "One month, a little more."

"Brave fellows."

"True that."

"And you as well. To marriage I refer."

Naoki laughed. "Kaeda the entire extravaganza apparently planning."

"And Chako?"

"Simple she prefers. Modern. No host dance party "

"Yabai! Behind that I can get!"

"And I. The rest to Kaeda I'll happily yield."

"To Kaeda I'd yield in a heartbeat. She's hot."

"Hotter than Chako?"

"Doro doro. Both. Differently hot."

"You Kaeda for a date should ask," Naoki grinned. "How hot you might then discover." He paused, then added, "Correct you might be."

"Concerning?"

"Waveweaver to ask." Naoki scooted back across the dock to lean against a piling and closed his eyes. He directed his thoughts toward the dolphin.

"We sing, we sing, we sing."

"The tuna you can see?" he asked.

"Fish, fish, fish, fish, fish!"

The watery rush engulfed him and he felt the compression as his body plunged deeper into the sea. He could see the milling bluefin inside the netted enclosure. Down and down and down. The milling fish were concentrated about three meters below the surface with far fewer in the lower portion of the cage.

"Thank you Waveweaver!"

"Fish, fish, fish, fish, fish," came the reply. "Just beat it."

Naoki opened his eyes. "Takusan, the highest density of fish at three meters occurs. Far fewer above and below."

"So into the equation that factor we insert?"

"Correct."

"And to Professor Koichi we then explain?"

Naoki shook his head. "With difficulty."

Waveweaver connected again. "The tuna, the tuna, you keep them contained. Nets you have nets."

"Yes?"

"Boats you have boats."

"Yes?"

"Hooks you have hooks. Hands you have hands."

"Yes? What telling? Or asking?"

"What do you call these things?"

Naoki thought a moment. "Tools. And with hands, tools we use. Our lives to build. Our cities."

"If we had tools, tools, tools, tools, tools..."

"And if you had hands," he added.

"If we had tools we'd not kill noisemakers."

Naoki sighed at the obvious implication. Some estimates went as high as 1,000 cetaceans each day were dying in fishing nets. Every day, every year.

"If we had tools we'd share them."

"If you had hands, I'd share my tools, Waveweaver."

"But we have lives already," she sang back. "We have no need to build them. And cities, we have heard of cities. Annejoule spoke of Ville au Camp, a city beneath the water, a city of gods, a city of the dead. A city built by Agwe. But there is no city. So Agwe has no tools? Agwe has no hands?"

"Perhaps there is no Agwe," Naoki replied.

I know, I know, we know, we know,

We sing, we swim, we listen

Baby, baby, baby, Where did our love go?

Only one place, Fish, fish, fish, fish, fish.

Ca Ira, Haiti

Dimanche, 15 August, 2010

One and a half months into their project, the École des Dauphins students had cleared and furrowed and fertilized more than two acres of soil. Jeanine guided their efforts, and although it was well past the usual planting season, had encouraged them to put in greens, radishes and peas, as well as several rows of mirletons and manioc.

"The manioc won't grow enough for root harvest next spring, but you'll have more cuttings for next season," she'd explained. "And the mirletons are perennial. The vines will grow 15 meters and more. You'll need to build frames for them."

Although Jeanine insisted it was the wrong season for melons, Annejoule, remembering her promise to the landlord, had gone ahead and planted a few cantelope seeds as well.

It being the dry season, one of the principal daily chores was drawing water from a long disused well on Web's property. The water was sweet, though tinged with rust, and the women took turns hauling bucketsful to tender seedlings and the sprouting sticks of manioc.

Watching them at their chore, the elder woman assured them, "Once you've brought up the soil, it will hold more water. And with the spring rains, you won't need to pump at all."

They began to sort collected driftwood into firewood and trellis wood, and to construct supports for the mirletons from those longer, slimmer pieces.

"You make a trépied, with three poles, you see?" Jeanine demonstrated, tying the three together with monofilament fishing line gathered on the shore. "And then another, and another, and then crosspieces, like so." Soon enough young vines were curling and climbing the driftwood ladders.

Now they were eating fresh mustard and radishes with their rice and bean staple, and the peas had begun to set pods.

Web stopped by from time to time and nodded approvingly. "Annejoule, you amaze me."

"We couldn't do this without you, and I couldn't do this without them," she replied, gesturing toward the women in the field.

When the temperature climbed in mid-afternoon the group would gather in the shade for Dan-Dan's lessons. Fascinated with Haiti's history, Annejoule had urged him to start again, as he had with her, and between his informal lectures they took turns reading aloud from *A propos de l'histoire d'Haiti, saviez-vous que.*

"If we were the first nation to throw off slavery, how is it that we remain so poor? Didn't our ancestors claim the estates of the slave masters?" Ghislaine had asked.

Dan-Dan shook his head sadly, "Unfortunately it seems that some of those slaves had learned the masters' game too well. They took advantage of others and soon became masters themselves, in fact if not in name."

"Is Haiti really the poorest nation on earth?" Anieltha queried aloud.

"I haven't been everywhere, but I can assure you we are at least among the very poorest."

"And Japan?" Lucsenda had wondered.

"Among the very richest."

Well aware than a second check had arrived from Naoki, and that his charity was underwriting their school, Lucsenda observed, "We're lucky Annejoule has a Japanese anmore." Then, seeing Annejoule's frown, she added. "Perhaps we all have a Japanese boyfriend, at that."

"I'd settle for a Haitian one," Saraphina sighed. "Rich or not."

Kushimoto, Japan

Suiyōbi, 1 September, 2010

Naoki suddenly screamed in apparent pain. "No! No! No! No! No!" he gasped.

"What? Is what?" Chicako gripped his hand. "What?"

"Killed. Certain I am. Waveweaver dead. Her scream I heard. The spear I felt. Her daughter, Surfslider, I hear. Wailing beyond wailing. She is trapped."

"Where, Naoki?"

"Taiji. It must be."

"But Waveweaver not to go there knew."

"Others to warn, she said. Others must warned be."

"How then caught?"

"Dolphin killers cacaphony create. Metal in the sea banging from a hundred boats. Confusion among their prey to instill. Ah, Chako, my dolphin friend is gone. Gone." Naoki fell to his knees, then curled up on the floor, overcome with uncontrollable weeping. Chicako settled beside him, arm across his shoulder, choking back her own sobs of grief.

A long while later she whispered.

Darkness swallows darkness

Heart is broken

From it flows a sea of tears.

Ca Ira, Haiti

Mercredi, 1 September, 2010

Annejoule awoke with a low moan. Then louder, "Ah, no! No!" She shook her head to clear her thoughts. "Oh, no!"

"What is it my daughter?" Jeanine called out from her sleeping pad.

"Dolphins are dying. Naoki is in such pain. The dolphins he knows are being killed. He is feeling their death. Silver Singer and others are crying out all around the world. They are all sharing in the pain."

"Tell them to trust in Damballa, and Agwe. The gods have their plans."

Annejoule didn't contradict her elder, keeping her doubts to herself. She began to cry, feeling the terrible sadness of her dolphin friends. Their sorrow seemed to circle the planet, a storm wind wailing of loss, a current thrumming with painful death.

Then she thought she heard Naoki through the din. She was sure at least that it was human thought she percieved, lacking the sing-song of the cetaceans. But it seemed somehow feminine.

Darkness swallows darkness

Heart is broken

From it flows a sea of tears.

"Naoki, I hear you. My heart is with your heart. Your sadness is my sadness. Naoki, my friend."

Kushimoto, Japan

Doyōbi , 11 September, 2010

SRFSLDR FREE!

SHOICHI NOT

???

S+2 CAUGHT

Naoki quit texting and called. "What happened?" he asked as soon as Chicako answered.

"Police the three divers arrested. Headlamps to a watchman apparently their route betrayed."

"But to release subsequent. Surfslider at least free is swimming. Her happiness boundless seeming. And others."

"Shoichi after posting bail called. Fifteen they freed. All of the holding pens they opened."

"Charges serious are?"

"Breaking and entering. Theft. Serious, yes."

"Theft? What evidence?"

Chicako laughed. "Evidence escaped. Poof!"

"A trial ..."

"Months away, no doubt. Shoichi quite pleased, however."

"Why?"

"The entire business of drive and slaughter and marketing as whale meat on trial he says. Everyone will know. Denial impossible."

Naoki whistled. "Tashika! True that!"

Ca Ira, Haiti

Samedi, 16 October, 2010

Annejoule straightened, shook the dirt from her hands and surveyed the farm field. Lucsenda, Aneiltha, Marie and Modelaine were working with her, pulling weeds between the rows of now sturdy plants. The mirleton vines had covered their driftwood supports, blossomed and set fruit.

Seeing the small squash Modelaine had questioned Jeanine. "Aren't those chayotes?"

"That's the city name. All my life we have called them mirletons. But yes, the same plant."

The mustard and collards were lush now, the manioc leafing and branching, a second crop of peas was coming ripe and two long rows of pinto beans were climbing poles so fast she thought she could see them move.

Daphcar, Perpétue, Saraphina and Ghislaine were taking turns pumping and carrying water, laughing and singing as they worked.

Three and a half months into her school project she could hardly have been happier with the progress they had made. Naoki continued to send monthly checks, an unexpected support that had made much of what they'd accomplished possible. At the outset she hadn't realistically considered what it would cost to feed her students in the time before crops began to come in, and absent the Japanese charity she now realized the whole scheme would never have worked.

Her communication with her benefactor had become more and more direct since the night of his crisis. When she silently thanked him she clearly heard his mental replies.

"How is the school doing?" he'd query.

"Oh, you should see the plants, Naoki. They are growing so very well. What news of Surfslider?"

"Often she visits, with her pod. Sadness evident, Waveweaver missing."

"So sad. Be well my friend."

Annejoule had noticed that these exchanges most often occurred in the early evening and mentioned it to Dan-Dan, which led to a class discussion of time zones and the International Date Line.

"It is fourteen hours later there than here," he'd explained. "The time zones were invented to rationalize travel and communications. If everyone used the same clock, the sun would rise at 6 a.m. in Haiti and at 8 p.m. in Japan."

"It still doesn't make great sense to me," Marie offered. "I mean, I get it, sort of."

"In any case, the reason Annejoule connects with Naoki most easily in the evening is that it is morning in Japan. And if people didn't create the Date Line, it would always be the same day, which would make no sense at all."

"That reminds me of one of my earliest communications with Silver Singer," Annejoule offered. "The dolphins don't understand time. They don't know about the earth turning. About the earth circling the sun. And they told me there is only one day."

Dan-Dan answered, "Life is very different for a weightless creature without technology." Then he added, "And for creatures who can communicate through their thoughts."

Once a week the women would go to the shore to swim with the dolphins, and return carrying the fish that their aquatic friends continued to supply.

Floating in the warm water of the bay, Perpétue had noted, "Dan-Dan is right. It would be very, very different to be weightless."

Kushimoto, Japan,

Doyōbi , 30 October, 2010

"Naokisan often with her speaks."

Kaeda shook her head. "Imagining difficult remains. And her story?"

Chicako thought for a few moments before answering. "Nine women apparently, farm techniques studying. Scholarly lessons as well. A retired professor instructing. One a baby expecting."

"Like your sister! About a niece excited?"

Leaning her chin on both elbows, Chicako replied. "Little girls not long ago we were. Now Kotone a mother to be, and I a bride." She sighed.

"Unhappy, gaarufureendo?"

"Wistful my childhood concerning."

"Before your parents died."

"That, surely. About the ways my life would different have been, I sometimes wonder. Not that the years with Oji Yam have unhappy been. But surely different."

"And now with Naoki."

"True. Would we have met? Would I love with a dear, dear heart have found? Desire for alternative pasts our current joy denies. And so, wistful, but not entirely regretting.

"There remains, ever, the innocence lost. A haiku online last night I read." She pulled out her cell, and clicked to the site.

"By a 'Lunicwolf.' Strange name. Innocence the title." She turned the screen to Kaeda.

Absolute beauty

Moonlight covers her pale face

Forever crying.

"The brutality in Taiji often crying incites."

Kaeda touched her arm. "But action you are taking. Changes will come."

Ca Ira,Haiti

Samedi, 30 October, 2010

"Dan-Dan, is there a word 'heisenberg?'" Annejoule had had to screw up her courage to ask the question, uncertain of what possible sexual implications it might have.

"Heisenberg was a scientist. In the last century. Why do you ask?"

"I've heard it in my," she almost said "dreams," which was true, but seemed too intimate to reveal, given the nature of the recurring experience. "In my talk with the dolphins."

"Heisenberg came up with an idea about uncertainty. I'm afraid I'm a historian, not a scientist, but the basic idea had something to do with measurement of location and speed."

"What was the uncertain part?"

Dan-Dan scratched his chin. "Something about," he paused, "I think. I mean, I guess I'm pretty uncertain about it myself. But something about not being able to determine where something is and how fast it is going at the same time." He smiled and added, "If the dolphins are discussing Heisenberg, perhaps you can ask them."

Kushimoto, Japan,

Nichiyōbi , 31 October, 2010

"Access to DNA testing you have?"

Naoki looked up, "Sure, Chako. Why?"

"Shoichi purchase of whale meat in Kushimoto requested. Testing to do."

They were sitting on a blanket in their cove. Surfslider and her pod were circling near its mouth.

"Ah. Proof that would be."

"Testing expensive?" Chicako wondered.

"Auspices of university, justification possible. Evidence for use in trial?"

"Exactly."

Naoki thought for a few moments, then, "Hey, upon consideration, Professor Saito, biochemistry instructor Higashiosaka City campus, DNA research conducting. My professor last year, and a good friend. Free testing, most likely."

"Shopping now?" Chicako began to rise.

Naoki caught her hand and tugged her back down. "Shopping later," he suggested, and pulled her into an embrace.

Surfslider I am! Daughter of Waveweaver.

We sing, we sing, we sing the silver sea!

Tools, tools, tools, tools, tools,

Baby, you're a firework

Come on, let your colors burst

Squidapple, squideemish, squiddiddle,

We sing, we sing, we sing.

La Siren, La Balenn,

Chapo'm tonbe nan la me.

La Siren, La Balenn,

Chapo'm tonbe nan la me.

"Now the dolphins in French are singing," he said.

"Haitian Creole, more likely," Chicako corrected.

"Usually the voices in Japanese I understand, but this different is."

Toward evening having returned to Naoki's apartment with several wrapped parcels of "whale" meat, Chicako booted his computer. "The Creole to translate," she explained.

After several attempts without success, Chicako typed the first four words into a search engine, making a phonetic stab at the spelling, and came up with a page of lyrics.

La Siren, La Balenn,

Chapo'm tonbe nan la me.

Clicking a button, a woman's voice sang the song.

"That's it!" Naoki exclaimed. "Now translate?"

Chicako copied it into a translator.

Sirens, Balenn, I want a hat from the sandbar.

"Nonsense." Naoki shook his head. "Another ad jingle that must be."

"Boifureendo, too hasty you are," Chicako laughed. "Sirens Greek mythology inhabit, half woman, half bird. Sea nymphs they are. Balenn a reference to baleen apparent seems, the source considering."

"Whales," Naoki murmurred. "And the hat?"

"Hmm." She ran the original back and forth through the translator, first to English, then to Japanese, then back to Creole. The meaning seemed to shift. "A hat" became "sis" became "six."

"Nonsense again?" Naoki sighed.

"Sirens unwary sailors lure, perhaps unwary whales as well? As a ship to the rocks, a whale to the sandbar?"

"I want away from the sandbar?"

"A song of freedom to me it seems. 'I shall be released.'"

Ca Ira, Haiti

Lundi, 1 November, 2010

Lucsenda had caught a ride to Léogâne with Dan-Dan on Saturday afternoon and two days later walked back into camp with Stanley. Handsome but shy, he was immediately the object of the students' attention and seemed a little embarrassed by all the fuss.

"We're going to marry!" Lucsenda announced jubilantly.

Stanley nodded. "Soon."

"And Stanley has an idea!" Lucsenda added. "For our farm!"

Annejoule cocked her head. "We always want new ideas. What's yours?"

The young man stuttered a bit as he began his reply. "I, I don't mean to intrude. I, I, well I just had a thought."

"We're waiting," Ghislaine demanded. "Out with it!"

"I, I, well, my uncle he sells vegetables from a stand in Port au. And, and, well, Lucsenda tells me that your farm will grow lots of food next spring. And, and ..."

"Get to the point!" Ghislaine interrupted.

"He is," Lucsenda intervened. "Just listen!"

"Well, well, I've worked for my uncle. And I think we, I mean you, but I want to help, I mean I'm going to be a father, and, well, maybe we could have a stand."

Lucsenda bubbled up, "To sell the stuff we grow here."

"And to get food to the people," Annejoule added. "That sounds wonderful!"

"A woman with a baby could surely sell vegetables," Lucsenda offered.

Daphcar jibed, "Always trying to get out of hard work. That's my sis!"

Kushimoto, Japan

Suiyōbi, 17 November, 2010

"Takusan?"

"Okay. But future there does not reside." Kaeda sighed. "Twice out together we've been. No chemistry."

"Than Naoki less a romantic he seems."

"True that. Computer gaming and manga his only passions, beyond oceanography. Fisheries management. With a man to cuddle and 98Koshien discuss? Please. Or comics? Help!"

Chicako laughed. "Naoki my poetry accepts. And back to me in bed repeats ..."

"While you're ...?"

Chicako nodded, and giggled. "And after."

"Way beyond acceptance that goes. Lucky woman you are." Changing the subject somewhat, Kaeda announced, "The Kushimoto Royal Hotel I have reserved for the wedding. Doyōbi, 14 Gogatsu, 2011."

"Oh, Kaeda! Most elegant! Our budget within?"

"No host, cash bar, hotel facility free ... if"

"If what?"

"If hotel restaurant as caterer hired."

"Cost?"

"Competitive. Trust me. This will perfectly work." She grinned, "And Takusan upon kanpai insists!"

"Well, to Naoki Taku close is."

"A wedding toast baseball, manga and tuna extolling! Novel that will be. And now gaarufureendo, about the dress a conversation imperative becomes."

"Shopping I detest."

"Fortunate to have me you are. In Wakayama. A splendid wedding shop on our return from Morioka to visit."

Kushimoto, Japan

Doyōbi, 27 November, 2010

     Takusan's e-mail subject line read "Navy sonar" and the content had been pasted from a 2002 story in *New Scientist*.

"THE US Navy has admitted for the first time that the sonar used by its ships can injure whales and dolphins.

"In a joint report issued last month with the National Marine Fisheries Service, the Navy has accepted that its sonar caused the beaching of 16 whales in the northern Bahamas in March 2000. But it maintains that the whales were the victims of unusual circumstance. It says the animals were swimming in the confined waters of the Providence Channel, which uniquely concentrated a range of sonar sounds used in training exercises in the area.

"All the dead animals autopsied after the Navy exercises "had experienced some sort of trauma likely to be associated with pressure, an intense acoustic event, or an impulse, that led to their stranding and subsequent deaths," says the report."

     Naoki replied: Damn, damn, damn.

Ca Ira, Haiti

Lundi, 20 December, 2010

Lucsenda moaned. "Mon bebe! He is ready!" She was weeping and laughing at the same time. She was squatting in the campsite, massaging her belly, and she groaned again as another contraction swept through her.

Daphcar jumped up. "I'm going for the midwife!" She bolted down the footpath toward town.

"Should we send for Stanley?" Anieltha wondered aloud.

Ghislaine laughed, "Men are no help with childbirth. He'd just be in the way!"

"I think you're supposed to walk around," suggested Saraphina. "That's what Mama always said."

"That's so," Modelaine affirmed.

Lucsenda stood, groaning, and began to pace. Shortly she squatted again. "I don't know about that." Then another deep sigh. "Oh, he wants to be born!" And louder, "I'm going to have a baby!" She broke into laughter, tears still streaming down her face.

It was a full hour before two midwives came puffing into camp, carrying a large galvanized steel washtub. One sat with Lucsenda and began to meaure her contractions in breaths and sighs. The other spread out soap, herbs and lotions and clean cloths on the dining table. "We'll need clean hot water," she announced. "Everything must be clean for the baby!"

Ghislaine gestured and asked, "What's the tub for?"

"For the three baths," one of the women replied.

Before long they had settled Lucsenda in one of the tents, lying on freshly laundered sheets. The other women, pacing or seated, laughed excitedly and chatted about the pending birth. From within the tent they heard a midwife quietly repeating, "Poussez! Poussez." The dog looked puzzled by the strange voice calling her name. She cocked her head and gazed toward the sound.

"Lucsenda is certain the baby is a boy."

"She hopes, you mean."

"Silver Singer confirmed."

"You're going to be an aunt, Daphcar!"

Jeanine arrived, beaming. She held aloft a string of tiny beads. "For the bebe!" she announced. "To ward off evil while her soul settles in." Then, producing a colorful cloth band, "And this to tie around his middle to make him strong."

"So you know it's going to be a boy, Jeanine?" Ghislaine asked.

"From the way Lucsenda carried herself these last weeks, it is certainly a boy."

"What are the three baths? One of the midwives spoke of that."

"After the birth, Lucsenda will take hot baths for three days, with healing herbs in the water. That's the first bath. The next three days she should bathe in herbal water warmed by the sun. That is the second bath and it is important for her to draw strength from Bondyè."

"And the third?"

"When the bebe is one month old, Lucsenda should take the third, cold, bath. It will help healing and tighten her joints and muscles that are just now being loosened by delivery."

A groan emanated from the tent, underscoring Jeanine's diagnosis. And then, much louder, "Oh my God!"

Followed in what seemed no time at all by the sound of an infant's wailing cry.

Kushimoto, Japan

Getsuyōbi, 20 December, 2010

SHOICHI TRIAL SET

??

14 YAYOI

2 WKS B4 MY GRAD

8 WKS B4 UR WED

:) OUR WED

:D

I'LL ATND TRIAL

??

RTRN FR SIS/BABY

GOT IT.

C U SNDY?

!!!!!!!!!!!!YESSSSSS

HSNBRG ME, BBY!

Naoki turned off his cell and stretched out, his head on the makura. Surfslider's voice came through as he relaxed toward sleep and then a chorus of other dolphin voices. Pop songs again.

Oh, na, na, what's my name?

Oh, na, na, what's my name?

What's my name? what's my name?

Surfslider Waveweaver's daughter

I slide the surf I sing the sea

Oh, na, na, what's my name?

Tools, tools, tools, tools, tools

If we had tools we'd build utopia

Naoki wondered aloud, or at least in his thoughts, "How would you do that, Surfslider? How would you build utopia?"

I'd like to teach the world to sing

To share, to share, to share

And that made some sense. So many of the core problems in the world seemed to emanate from greed, from inability to share. Perhaps the dolphins could generate a better plan.

We sing, we sing, we sing the silver sea.

Ca Ira, Haiti

Mercredi, 22 December, 2010

Lucsenda held the newborn to her breast, lying propped up in the tent where she'd given birth. The other students were taking turns visiting with her, admiring the boy, and wanting to do more than was needed for the new mother.

"Dan-Dan has gone to tell Stanley. He'll be so proud! And your parents if he can find them in the camp."

"That's true. I hope he can come here soon. And Maman. She's a grandmother now."

"When will you name him?"

"In my family, we always wait a month."

"Tradition?"

"To see if they survive. So many babies are not strong enough for this world."

"This one will live. Your diet has been good. You're healthy. And you ate red fruit these last two months. That has made his blood strong."

"I am filled with hope."

When Annejoule was sitting beside her friend she reported, "Silver Singer is eager to meet your new one. She is excited for you, and for all of us. She calls us her noisemaker family."

"Soon enough, we'll take mon bebe down to the sea."

Laban peered at his new cousin, wide-eyed and wondering. He reached across and gently touched the child's cheek. "So little! Was I ever so small?"

"I remember when you were!" Annejoule replied.

"And with maman?"

Pulling him into her embrace she answered again. "Yes, with your wonderful maman, Marianne. And Marianne is the reason you are so smart and handsome, Laban."

The toddler smiled up at her, then reached out again to touch the newborn's toe. "So little!"

Kushimoto, Japan

Doyōbi, 15 January, 2011

"Tomorrow the anniversary of the Haitian earthquake will be." Naoki and Chicako strolled along the wharf, enjoying the first sunny day of the week.

"To fathom such destruction difficult is." She paused and added, "Naokisan, a people to such devastation pursuant, how hope to reclaim?"

"Forward looking, not back, I think. A cause discovering. A world to rebuild."

"Annejoule that doing is. A new world growing."

"And collective at that. Annejoule with the money here raised, tools has purchased, for all to use." Naoki added, "Dolphins of tools now sing. And of the perfect and shared world if tools they possessed building they would be."

"Socialism the sea within?"

"So it seems. A baby's birth hope as well instills."

"Five weeks now, an aunt I will be!"

"Chako, old enough an aunt to be you are not," murmured Naoki, extending an arm and drawing her into an embrace. "When again your travel date?"

"Old enough memory loss to have you are not! 5 Yayoi. 5 Yayoi. Got it? 11 Yayoi to Wakayama therafter. For wedding dress shopping. Shoichi's trial on Monday to attend. 15 Yayoi to you I return."

"Soon enough never will it be." He hugged her more

tightly and kissed her hair. "A long rail journey that is."

"Nine hours up. Six to Wakayama the bullet riding. Two home."

"And Kaeda?"

Chicako poked him in the stomach with one finger. "Yes, silly. You a dozen times I've told. My shopping queen."

"Alone I would worry."

"Alone I will not be."

Ca Ira, Haiti

Dimanche, 16 January, 2011

"A year today." Annejoule looked around the campfire at the other students. "A sorrowful, and yet, a hopeful year."

"Everything changed," Perpétue offered.

Ghislaine countered, "And so much that did not. Misery added to poverty, and the poverty always pervasive."

"In remembrance I'd suggest we share the names of those we lost," Perpétue murmured. "My grandmother, Maneeya, and my uncle Belensky. In Port au."

"My best friend, Naitana, in Léogâne. And her parents," intoned Marie. "And her brother."

"Stevenson, Shelove, Murielle, Ritha and Kelly, in Port au," Ghislaine recalled. "And Stevenson's son, Darly. He died of the cholera just this fall."

Annejoule spoke quietly, "Mon Maman, Annabelle, and my little brother, Justinien. Buried in our apartment block."

"I so well remember my Aunt Mathenia. She always made us laugh," Lucsenda smiled. Then more somberly, "She and my Uncle Jeff-Herson. Both took the cholera, in Port au. And my cousins Nerlande, Nastassia and Mergena. Also this fall. The cholera is so dreadful."

"We are lucky to be outside the city," Marie observed. "Thanks to you, Annejoule."

Daphcar agreed, "Yes, thanks to Annejoule, we're away from the filth and disease. Mon Pere, was so badly injured in the quake, that he's had a long recovery. Finally, just lately, he is able to work again. But it has been a very hard year for my family. They were happy for Lucsenda and me to come here, not just for the chance to learn, but to lighten the load at home. Maman has struggled to care for our young brothers."

On the remembrance continued, into the late evening. So many gone, so deep the suffering, so much that was lost.

Kushimoto, Japan

Suiyōbi, 20 January, 2011

"Taku, Kaeda of wedding plans to you has spoken?"

"Twice. Your humble Takusan clearly not Kaeda's favor enjoying. But, the toast at least she myself has accorded."

Naoki laughed. "Chako Kaeda's noninterest in 98Koshien and manga mentioned. Other subjects of conversation you might consider."

The friends shoveled mackerel to swirling bluefins as they conversed. The fish had grown quickly over the past year and the surface of the enclosure was shot through with trails of speeding dorsal fins. The ultramarine backs of the feeding tuna crested clear of the water as they carved through the mass of chopped fish.

"To market soon," commented Naoki. "Crowding to relieve."

Takusan reverted to the previous subject. "Women I understand not."

"Understanding of small consequence. Empathy a long distance travels. Pretty woman a sword cutting life is. Your guard you might put down."

"Then cut to be?"

"To the heart, my friend. To the heart."

The pair worked in silence for a while as Takusan considered the advice. Finally he said, "Try I can."

"Kaeda concerning wedding plan details you could ask.

Interest in her interests showing."

"In seeing her naked body greater interest holds ..."

Naoki laughed aloud again. "Against making such a request I'd recommend, if actually her body seeing naked your goal is."

Feeding complete they washed down the wheelbarrows and shovels, stowed them and went inside to attend to the latest batch of fry in their long glass aquaria. The steady hiss of aerators and filters lent a churchlike sense of calm to the hatchery, and they spoke in lower voices as they repeated their earlier chore on a tiny scale. Three-centimeter-long hatchlings swarmed the spoonsful of brine shrimp ladled into their midst.

"About what should I talk?"

"Now?"

"With Kaeda, time to make."

"Chako of Kaeda's painting has spoken. Ink and watercolor."

Takusan shook his head. "Of painting little I know."

"Better still. The student you can be. For explanation allowing. Most interesting others interested in ourselves we find."

"Interested in her interest I am."

Naoki shook his head laughing. "Certain of that I am. Another bit of advice. A meal for her you might cook."

"Me? Cook?"

"Sushi and noodles. Simple but impressive. Intent the principal goal. Your concern for reasonable nutrition to show."

Ca Ira, Haiti

Vendredi, 18 February, 2011

Jeanine had announced that it was time to start planning for the first full garden season and the women were clustered around her offering suggestions and considering her advice. Since their start in July, the students had worked up more than two acres of soil, double-digging the rows and burying jellyfish as they filled them in again. Compost piles sent up steam on cool mornings, and the manioc and mirletons were lush with new growth.

"Two considerations to keep in mind," the elder explained, "are what grows well here, and what the market might be. For instance, the mirletons are so easy to grow that the market value isn't high. It's good to have them as a staple, and no harm in offering them at Lucsenda's stand, but other crops will bring more money."

"Manioc seems easy too," Ghislaine observed.

"It is, but the advantage with manioc is that it can be dried and used or sold over a long period. So storage is a third consideration. Carrots, for example, don't fade so quickly as fruits like tomatoes."

"The choices seem hard," Anieltha commented. "How do we decide?"

"Diversity is the wisest course, because even the crops that grow well here may grow differently from one season to the next. The pests may be worse, or the wilt."

Annejoule spoke up, "I've noticed from the first time I was in your garden, Jeanine, that you alternate rows."

"Quite right. If one plants different crops from row to row, it confuses the bugs, and you're less likely to lose all of one crop to an infestation. Of course, with all of you," she gestured around the circle, "working the field, the bugs won't have much of a chance!"

Kushimoto, Japan

Doyōbi, 19 February, 2011

DNNR I MADE 4 KAEDA!

CHEF U R

KAEDA PNTNGS SHWD!

TLD U SO

SHKIBTN/MKURA SHARED!

2 MCH INFO

KAEDA HOT!

2 MCH INFO

IN BED HOT!

WAY 2 MCH INFO

Ca Ira, Haiti

Lundi, 21 February, 2011

Ghislaine dragged a small stick through soft soil to form a shallow trench while Anieltha carefully planted tiny carrot seeds and sprinkled fine soil over them.

"Do you ever wonder why no one else can hear the dolphins? They certainly seem friendly enough."

Ghislaine pursed her lips and tapped her cheek with an index finger before answering. "Well, she was unconscious after her building collapsed. She was hit pretty hard on the head."

"I would so like to hear them. Maybe I'll club myself with a shovel handle. I wonder if that would work."

"I'm not that curious, myself." Ghislaine laughed, "Not enough to knock myself out. And then the Japanese man apparently fell off a bicycle and hit his head, at least according to Annejoule. So same difference."

"It all seems so much like magic."

"Strange, yes. But not as magical as those itsy seeds you're planting turning into carrots, or those chopped off twigs we planted growing into manioc bushes as tall as you. That's real magic, I think."

"Do you pray, Ghislaine?"

"I used to."

"But now?

"No. Annejoule and Dan-Dan have pretty well convinced me it's a waste of time."

"Because?"

"Because there's nobody listening. If there is a God, or gods, either he doesn't care about Haiti or has no power to make anything better. No god I can believe in would consign so many to hunger, to poverty, to disease. For what? For having sex? For seeing each other naked?"

"But what made the world then?"

"Maybe it's just always been."

"Things have to be made, somehow, I think. Don't they?"

"So the preachers say. When I came here last summer, I still believed what I'd heard in church. But thinking through all I've learned from Dan-Dan, from the garden, from the dolphins and from Jeanine ..."

"Jeanine still believes in the voudoo ..."

"Yeah. But her garden lessons make more sense as science than the work of Agwe." Ghislaine thought a bit, then, "And you see the problem with saying 'God made the world,' or 'Damballa made the world,' always comes around to, 'Okay then, who made God?'"

Anieltha finished the row of seeds and sat back. "Well, I guess I just thought God always existed."

"You see where that leads, right? Is that any different than saying the world always existed? I don't think that suggests I should pray to the world."

"No. I guess not."

"Which brings me back to the poverty and disease and accidents and earthquakes and all the rest. If I were sure there was a God out there somewhere, I don't think I'd like him. I sure wouldn't believe he liked me. Where was he when I was gang-raped?"

Anieltha shook her head. "True enough. And you were praying back then." She stood, brushing dirt off her hands. "I still do, I guess because of mon maman. She always told me to pray every night. But ... " Here she bit her lip and looked straight into her friend's eyes. "But the truth is, I can't say I ever got anything I prayed for, I mean, anything that wasn't obviously going to happen anyway."

Ghislaine laughed again. "Like praying the sun will come up tomorrow?"

"That too," she responded, grinning. "If the serious prayers had worked I'd have fourteen rich boyfriends by now!" Then, somberly, "And none of my friends would have died from the cholera."

Shingu, Japan

Kayōbi, 22 February 2011

Following dinner on their first double-date the four friends had seen *Noruwei no mori*. The film was a dramatic romance whose events spun out from a man's memories triggered by hearing the title song, the Beatle's "Norwegian Wood," a friend's suicide in the 60's and his subsequent friendship with that suicide's girlfriend, named Naoku. The suicide shattered Naoku's already fragile spirit, and her depression landed her in a sanitorium.

Chicako and Kaeda were reduced to tears more than once during the show.

"Grim was that," Naoki said as they exited the theater.

"Dark," added Takusan.

"Such tragedy," Kaeda observed. "Naoku without hope, and his life not really better. His attempts at romance miserably failed!"

Taku took the opportunity to suggest, "Seeing *Autoreiji,* instead, perhaps better?"

"Not mafia. No," Chicako shivered. "Enough violence the news within, for violent movies on my part no need."

They rehashed the plot during the 45 minute drive home, and Chicako pulled close to Naoki in the back seat. She whispered, "Absent your love, Naokisan, a Naoku I'd be."

He kissed her and interlaced his fingers with hers. "Here I will remain," he assured her. Then to Taku, "Your father a kind man his car to loan."

"Gruff but generous he is."

Chicako noticed that the pair in the front seat were holding hands. She nudged Naoki and pointed, then winked at him.

Their conversations wandered as Taku drove, laughing and joking until they passed through Taiji, when the grim mood that had followed the film recurred.

"Captives in the pens hearing I am," Naoki muttered, weariness and heartache in his voice.

Kaeda answered, "More I wish we could do."

"The court case coming," Chicako replied. "Perhaps the evidence Shoichi offers, the DNA tests the university from, perhaps ... "

"We can hope," Naoki sighed. "We can only hope."

Ca Ira, Haiti

Vendredi, 25 February, 2011

"What's your Japanese anmore like?" Anieltha couldn't resist tweaking Annejoule.

Refusing to rise to the bait, her friend ignored the dig and thought a few moments before responding. "He seems very kind. His generosity is obvious, I guess, from the money he sends us for the school. He seems to be very smart, and studying at a university. Something to do with fish. Oceanography. That's it. Oceanography. I guess he studies the ocean. Oh, and he definitely has a girlfriend. Somewhere along the way I got the impression that they are going to marry soon. We don't exactly have conversations."

"Don't you hear him all the time now? Ghislaine seems to think so."

"No. Sometimes the communication is direct and clear, usually at times of high emotion." Annejoule wasn't going to go into details about the whens and whys of some of her experiences, which still exposed more of Naoki's intimate relationship with Chicako than she much wanted to know. "Other times, it's more of a general impression. He seems serious. Urgent about helping dolphins being killed by Japanese fishermen. And ... " she paused, then repeated what she'd offered at the outset. "And he seems to be very, very kind."

Kushimoto, Japan

Doyobi, 5 March, 2011

Naoki and Takusan had accompanied Chicako and Kaeda to the train station early in the day, then waved as the brakes released and the cars jerked forward into smooth motion.

Having observed his friend's lengthy parting embrace and effusive chatter, Naoki teased, "Much warmer your relationship with Kaeda appears."

"And you to thank I have. Her paintings."

"A long week this will be."

"Some studying I may achieve."

"Finals soon. Kaeda's absence your GPA may salvage!"

"True that."

Naoki's cell beeped and he looked to see a text from Chicako.

THOSE 2!

HOT&HVY!

:-D

TAKU LNLY ALRDY

KAEDA MOONY

YNG LVE

MISS U MUCH

MS U MORE!

Kushimoto, Japan

Suiyōbi, 9 March, 2011

Chicako's messages during the week consisted mostly of dozens of photos of her newborn niece, interspersed with brief exclamatory bursts.

2 CUTE!!!!!

SO TINY!!!!

WHT A DOLL!!!!!

There were pictures of Chicako and Kaeda holding the infant, dozens of Kotone and her husband gazing fondly at the little one, and more brief exclamations.

SO HPY!:-)

SWT BBY!!!!

Occasionally interspersed were countdowns that cheered him considerably. 5 DAYS, 4 DAYS, 3 DAYS ... that made Naoki feel a bit more missed, though he told himself that he needn't long for such acknowledgment.

Then a longer message that brought Naoki up short.

SN WE HVE BBY 2!

For a sobering instant he contemplated the possibility of his girlfriend's pregnancy, which he doubted, but could easily deem possible. Then he pondered the longer-range prospect of marriage and, he assumed, parenting at some point, though that seemed a distant future decision. The pending marriage seemed serious enough on its own without dwelling overmuch on bigger responsibilities that lay ahead. But, if Chako was indeed expecting and ready for motherhood, he decided he could roll with that too.

He replied. PREG WE R?

HA HA HA HA SWT SLLY MAN! NO!

U SAY SOON

DRMING MY LVE! LVE U SO!

ME U 2! C U SN!!!!

Ca Ira, Haiti

Mardi, 8 March 2011

Stanley now spent two or three days a week helping with the farm, and today he'd arrived with two friends, announcing his intention to greatly increase the composting effort.

The women gathered around and he made introductions. "These are my good buddies, Jean Caleb and Olventz. I've told them about your Ecole des Dauphins and they wanted to help out."

"And meet you," added Olventz, smiling broadly, and looking around the circle. "We brought a tent."

Ghislaine nudged Anieltha and whispered in her ear, barely suppressing a giggle. "Maybe your prayers worked."

"They don't look rich," was the whispered and giggled response.

In short order the three young men had turned the established compost piles. Meanwhile Annejoule and Perpetué had rowed out with the seine and begun hauling in another load of jellyfish.

Stanley and Jean Caleb made quick work of hauling the bulging net to shore, and joined in tossing bait fish to the trailing dolphins.

"I understand the name," Jean Caleb said, nodding. "Beautiful creatures."

Then as the men began to load and haul the catch, the two women went back out for another load.

"It's nice having strong men to help," Perpetué commented as she pulled on the oars.

"We're all pretty strong ourselves," Annejoule retorted. "I hope they are the same sort as Stanley. Ghislaine and I aren't the only women assaulted in Léogâne. My trust level is low."

"But surely Stanley wouldn't expose Lucsenda to men he didn't trust!"

"That's true."

"And they're both handsome."

"They're certainly helpful."

Perpetué grinned, "Well I hope they stick around."

"Could be complicated," sighed Annjoule. "Certainly could be."

Wakabayashi, Japan

Kin'yōbi, 11 March 2011

     BRDNG TRN 3 HRS

     WHN RCH WKYMA?

     6 PM

     THNK 2 JOIN U

     IN WKYMA?

     YES, 4 WKND

     TAKU 2?

     THNK YES

     KAEDA WLL LIK

     +U?

     CHAKO WLL LOV! KAEDA'S UNCL VRY ILL

     SRRY TO HR, C U SN!!!!

Ca Ira, Haiti

Vendredi, 11 March, 2011

Annejoule lay awake. It had to be past midnight, because she knew she'd slept a while. Silver Singer and other dolphins were clearly upset, but the upset itself was unclear. Something about motion in the water.

Swim, swim, swim, swim, swim.

Swim away, swim away, swim away

It seemed to be a warning to others of some imminent danger. And then she could also sense Naoki's thoughts. He too was worried about something not right.

Kushimoto, Japan

Kin'yōbi, 11 March, 2011

"Something wrong is." Naoki sat down hard on a bench. He and Takusan had just purchased tickets to Wakayama and were waiting in the crowded station for the next train, which would depart shortly after 3 p.m. The coming weekend meant the commuter run would be packed.

"Wrong?"

"Surfslider extremely upset."

"About?"

"Movement. Water moving. Shaking."

"And?"

"Understanding evades. But very upset. Now hearing 'Trapped, trapped, trapped. Rolling, rolling, rolling!' Bang, bang, bang!' But Surfslider not the one trapped. Very strange."

Takusan pulled his cell out and clicked it open to see a message from Kaeda.

WATER!

YES? he replied. But there was no response.

Naoki opened his own phone to a partial message from Chicako.

VALNT DRMR I LVE... He too received no answer to his quickly typed reply.

Both men sent repeated texts to no avail over the next quarter hour. Then a sober-voiced announcement blared through the station on the public address system.

"All trains on all routes cancelled. More information soon."

The friends spotted a cluster of commuters gathered in front of a large television monitor and pushed their way through to view the screen. The newscaster, visibly shaken, gestured toward a large map of the northeast coast, and above the noise of the crowd, they heard the words "tsunami" and "with bullet train contact lost—Morioka and Fukishima between" and "2:46 p.m."

The friends turned to each other in fearful realization. "The bullet to ride they planned," Naoki whispered. His chin began to quiver, he looked down, swallowed hard, and then pulled out his cell and began furiously texting.

Takusan hurried toward an information kiosk, but found himself unable to push through the gathering throng. There were angry shouts from some whose travel plans had been suddenly cut short, others were silently staring at train schedules, and more than a few were weeping in an openly public display of emotion rarely witnessed among generally staid Japanese.

Naoki gave up his attempt to reach Chicako and phoned her sister, Kotone. "Which train?"

"The bullet, I think, but ..."

"Oh. Kotone! No!" He could say no more, sat straight down on the pavement, and cried, hope draining from his thoughts with each wracking sob. "Oh, Chako. Oh, Chako."

Much later, Naoki rode his bicycle away from the station, down past the harbor and the bridge, through the tunnel and out to the cove trail. He threw down his bike, and walked slowly down to the sea.

Ca Ira, Haiti

Vendredi, 11 March, 2011

Sweat was streaming down Annejoule's face as she worked a pitchfork, emptying a wheelbarrow full of weeds onto the recently built compost pile.

She stopped short, overwhelmed by a sense of disaster. The something wrong she'd sensed during the night was very, very wrong. Some sort of terrible disaster had happened.

Naoki's voice, or, rather, his thoughts the way she heard them, were abruptly very clear.

"Chako is dead. My Chako is dead. My Chako is dead." Over and over he repeated the thought.

"Dear Naoki. Poor Naoki. I am so, so saddened. What is it that happened?"

All she could understand was a powerful sense of bottomless grief, and his repetition that the love of his life was gone. She stuck the pitchfork into the mound before her, and walked quickly to Dan-Dan's home.

"Dan-Dan, something terrible has happened in Japan. Have you heard anything?"

"No. But I'll call Fedji."

After a brief conversation, Dan-Dan hung up his phone and said, "A tsunami has struck Japan."

When her blank look revealed a lack of comprehension, he added, "When there is an earthquake beneath the ocean, it can cause a massive wave that can do immeasurable damage. That's called a tidal wave or a tsunami. Fedji says reports indicate a huge wave has struck Japan's east coast, and that many thousands are feared dead."

"I fear Naoki's fiancé has perished as well. He is terribly, terribly distraught."

"We know earthquakes all too well," her teacher added.

Kushimoto, Japan

Doyōbi, 12 March, 2011

Naoki had sat on the rocks, staring into the lapping waves, by turns crying or still, remembering and aching. He was so lost in thought, and so completely adrift, that he was startled when the sky began to lighten and the first fingernail of sun appeared on the eastern horizon.

He tapped his phone awake, and clicked to a news site.

Thousands dead.

Radiation leak at Fukushima Daiichi power station.

EJR affirms bullet train not lost.

He tried Chicako's number again, then Takusan's, and reaching neither, jogged back to where he'd left his bike, and raced toward home.

Later, seated in front of his computer, he sped from Web site to Web site, keeping multiple tabs open to follow breaking news.

The East Japan Railway continued to deny the loss of any trains, but aerial video cameras showed scenes of derailed train cars scattered chock-a-block amidst wrecked automobiles and trucks, the mounded remains of splintered frame buildings, trees, boats and unidentifiable flotsam.

Radiation continued to leak from the Fukishima reactors, and pressure was said to be building within the containment structures. Electricity was out in a wide area, TEPCO was asking customers to conserve power, and cell phone service was out over much of the northeast coast.

A text message came in from Shoichi.

CAPTVE DOLPH TAIJI INJRD N CGES

DAMN THEM!

His phone beeped.

"About the train you heard?"

"Yes, Taku. Safe they may be."

"Disaster exceeds belief."

"And so very difficult not knowing. Shoichi texted that captive dolphins in Taiji injured were. One small tragedy the many among."

"You'll let me know if from Kaeda and Chako you hear?"

"Of course."

Hours passed, with an endless repetition of scenes from various news channels. A video shot with a cell phone from a hotel balcony showed large ships washed over a sea wall, canting on their sides and crashing into buildings and bridges. Another followed a wall of water surging across small farm fields, lifting homes, cars, building materials, bagged garbage, and more in an inexorable black flood. Then back to the scattered train cars, which were clearly not the sleek coaches of a bullet train, reports that all aboard a commuter train had died, and again to denials from EJR.

Exhausted and famished after his sleepless night and hours in front of his Mac, Naoki finally ate the lunch he'd packed for the planned trip to Wakayama and collapsed on his shikibuton, not bothering to shed his clothes.

Ca Ira, Haiti

Samedi, 12 March 2011

Dan-Dan had connected via phone with a colleague in Port au who relayed more of the news flowing in from Japan.

"Perhaps tens of thousands are dead there," he told the assembled women. "The earthquake was as powerful as ours a year ago, only it happened off the coast and created a wave that destroyed ships, houses, hotels, trains, cars, trucks, everything. It swept everything before it. And to make everything much worse, a nuclear power plant has been severely damaged and radiation is spreading. People are being evacuated."

"Nuclear? Radiation?" Anieltha queried.

This led to a long discussion of nuclear energy, a subject new to all of the students. Dan-Dan simplified it to the extent possible, but in the course of an hour's discussion they all understood, at least, that this nuclear energy created heat which was used to make steam, which was used to power turbines, and that the stuff that burned in a nuclear reactor was terribly, terribly poisonous.

Annejoule had only half listened, seated with her back to a wall, tuned in to dolphin chatter which had settled into its normal sing-song calm. Suddenly she blurted, "Now Naoki thinks Chicako escaped unharmed. Her train was safe."

Kushimoto, Japan

Nichiyōbi, 13 March, 2011

Naoki awoke early and immediately turned on his computer again. Shoichi had forwarded a Wikipedia entry.

Report, March 13

Speaking of Taiji, we learned today that the tsunami came there too. The fishing boats and molesters' boats took to sea to ride out the wave. No thought was given though to the dolphins trapped in the pens in the harbor. Six times, the water receded and returned, but did not flood the town. Six times, the captive dolphins were smashed against rocks and screamed in agony. At least 24 of the dolphins perished. Any farmer would release livestock when confronted with a fire. The souls of the dolphin molesters are without light.

Naoki exhaled in a long sigh. His world was coming apart. How could he contain any more sadness?

Annejoule's thoughts came through.

"Naoki, I am with you. I feel your heartache."

"Annejoule, what am I to do? I don't know if my Chako is alive or dead. I am weary and sad and worried."

"Have you spoken with Chako's grandfather?"

He sat up. Why hadn't he thought of Oji Yamamoto? The elder must be as worried as he, and just as much alone.

"Thank you Annejoule. Thank you."

He shut down the computer and ran down the stairs. Soon he was riding toward Chicako's home.

Heart beating hard he knocked at the door, restraining himself from hammering out his urgency and worry. Soon he heard shuffled steps inside and the door opened to reveal the old man's sad visage. They bowed to each other.

"My boy, come in. Come in. The tea of sadness best alone not sampled."

"Hopeful I remain, Oji Yam. The bullet train unharmed ..."

The elder was silent and led the young man to the kitchen where a kettle was steaming on the stove. He turned off the burner and poured water into a small teapot, set it on the table, pulled two cups from a cupboard, and gestured toward cushions on the floor. "Let us sit."

"Naoki, my Chicako two days ago called."

"Me the train yesterday about to board she texted."

"From?"

"Morioka."

"Sadly, no. Kaeda and Chicako from original plans detoured. Thursday from Morioka they departed. To Sendai Shiogama Port they traveled, Kaeda's uncle to visit. The uncle most desperately ill."

"But Kotone the bullet train said ..."

"In Sendai yesterday to catch."

"And so safe she must be."

"Sendai Shiogama Port destroyed. The train she never reached."

Naoki's thoughts collapsed around him again. Tears welled up in his eyes, and Oji Yama reached across the table to touch his arm. "Gesshu Soko of this writes."

Inhale, exhale

Forward, back

Living, Dying:

Arrows, let flown each to each

Meet midway and slice

The void in aimless flight

Thus I return to the source.

Ca Ira, Haiti

Dimanche, 13 March, 2011

"Oh, poor Naoki." Annejoule whispered. "Such loss."

Kushimoto, Japan

Kayōbi, 15 March, 2011

Since phoning Takusan to relay Oji Yam's devastating news, Naoki had contacted no one. He sat in front of his monitor, playing and replaying video of the explosion at the Fukishima Daiichi reactor. The flames and smoke seemed to well illustrate the fracturing of his universe. Each day the situation seemed more dire. Warnings about tap water and contaminated food. The evacuation area widened. More and more graphic images of the utter destruction of whole towns.

He searched for images from Sendai Shiogama Port but found only a few specifically labeled as such. The estimated height of the tsunami water there was 8 meters, taller than the two story house where Kaeda's uncle doubtless perished as well. The port itself was a jumble of shipping containers and tractor-trailers. Ships that hadn't escaped to sea were sitting atop low buildings in some places. And astonishingly, the port authorities had announced that they'd resume operations the next day, at least for emergency efforts.

With five days remaining before his final examinations he could find no interest in studies. He felt hollowed out, drained of joy or any hope of joy, or any hope of hope.

Once again he watched the explosion, the fire, the smoke.

Once again he collapsed, exhausted and aching.

Surfslider's singing came through in the night.

Light de light, we got mornin',

mornin' makes another day,

We sing, we sing, we sing the silver sea.

Glory sight, got de dawnin'

Lordy, light the night away!

In the depths of the night he felt Annejoule, he sense her caring, he felt some comfort, and yet, mostly, he felt completely alone.

"Oh, my dear Chicako. Naoku I now am. Alone."

Ca Ira, Haiti

Vendredi, 18 March, 2011

"Reports out of Japan continue to worsen." Dan-Dan now offered daily updates to the young women, based on phone calls with acquaintances in the city. "There is fear that the damaged nuclear power plant may melt down completely. That means a catastrophic failure that could send poisonous radiation around the world. The danger from the radiation is so great that rescue crews can't even go to some places where people may still be alive, but trapped. It is desperately bad."

"And you said food and water are contaminated?" Ghislaine asked. "What will they do?"

"Clean water in bottles, and clean food from other parts of the country. But roads are still blocked and getting supplies to some areas remains impossible."

"The evacuation must look much like the tent camps outside Leogane," Lucsenda observed. "So many people displaced."

Ghislaine countered, "But less hunger and disease for them. They are rich. Hurting yes, but at least with more resources than we had here."

Dan-Dan turned to Annejoule, "And what news of Naoki?"

"All I can feel from him is heartache."

Kushimoto, Japan

Kayōbi, 22 March, 2011

  U MSSD EXAM

  DNT CARE

  FINALS!

  DNT CARE

  GRADUATION!

  CARE LSSS

  NAOKI! NOT QUIT!

  DNT CARE

Ca Ira, Haiti

Mercredi, 23 March, 2011

Jeanine had attempted to console Annejoule, whose depression tracked that of her distant correspondent.

"Agwe and the others have their plans, my daughter. It is not for us to know. Jeanine simply trusts."

"Naoki seems so broken. Even more than I felt concerning Maman and Justy, if that is possible. He seems so very alone."

"The only thing you can do for him is what I did for you, Annejoule."

"You fed me. You took me in. I can't do that for Naoki."

Jeanine enclosed Annejoule in her arms and hugged her close. "I loved you, my daughter. I gave you my love. It was love that fed you, and love that took you in."

Lying awake late that night, Annejoule tried to reach out to Naoki but could feel no thoughts from him.

"Silver Singer, can you get a message to Naoki?"

"Of course my friend."

"Tell Naoki Annejoule loves him."

Sing, we sing, we sing the silver sea

On and on we swim the golden waves

Love, love, love, I want your love.

Fish, fish, fish, fish, fish.

Love, love, love, love, love.

Wakabayashi, Japan

Nichiyōbi, 27 March, 2011

With the trains running again, Naoki had traveled to Sendai to see for himself the destruction that had broken his heart. At the train station he rented a bicycle and rode several miles to Wakabayashi. Kaeda's parents had corrected Oji Yam's information about the uncle's home, and extended internet searches had provided an address as well as more pictures of devastation, perhaps worse than the port, since more of the seaside area had been residential.

As he closed the distance, evidence of the earthquake and tsunami was everywhere. Jumbled piles of building materials and trailers loaded with emergency food rations and water lined the streets. Bits of styrofoam were strewn like confetti, mixed with mud on every surface. Fences were matted with plastic bags, hats, drinking straws, rope, ribbon. Gutters and sidewalks were piled with magazines, dolls, shingles, shredded clothing, ball point pens, dead fish, tires, flower pots, shoes, bent-up bicycles, lattice, brooms, cell phones, fish nets, and more plastic bags.

He looked again at the map on his cell, and turned off the main road for a few blocks then turned again. Despite it being Sunday, bulldozers and front-end loaders were plowing into the rubble in the increasingly damaged building blocks.

Ahead the land was still inundated, large pools of oily water had remained where no drainage had ever been needed before. The neat checkerboard of homes he'd seen in aerial photos was entirely gone. A yellow police tape crossed the road, with signs indicating that only emergency personnel were permitted beyond.

He locked the bike to a bent-over light pole, ducked under the ribbon, and walked two more blocks amid the wreckage, to the intersection where the house must have stood. The house where Chicako had stayed for her last night on earth.

There was nothing to be seen but a gaping foundation hole and a scattering of broken boards and shattered glass.

"To live I no longer desire, Chako."

He turned and slowly retraced his route, picking his way through stinking garbage and nail studded lumber, his tears adding a few more drops of salty water to the saturated landscape.

Ca Ira, Haiti

Mardi, 29 March, 2011

    "Live for me, Naoki. I love you." Annejoule repeated her message, a litany, as she worked, as she swam, as she cooked, as she picked hornworms from tomatoes and sliced borers from squash vines. "You I love. I wrap my love around you."

Kushimoto, Japan

Suiyōbi, 13 April, 2011

Though there had been a few desultory text messages from Naoki, Takusan hadn't seen his friend face-to-face since leaving the railway station in March. He'd offered invitations, suggested excursions, even knocked on the apartment door, but Naoki remained incommunicado.

Finally he'd hit on a plan. He knocked again. "Naoki I inside know you are. A check for the school I have, Kickstarter from." He waited. Finally there was movement and the knob turned.

"Okay. In you may come."

"Wretched you look. How much weight lost has been?" Takusan looked around and saw that most of his friend's possessions were missing, and that a stack of neatly taped boxes sat adjacent to the door. "Moving you are?"

"Leaving."

"For?"

"Haiti."

"That you can't do."

"Why not?"

"Well. Your career ..."

"What career?"

"About this your thinking thorough has been?"

"About nothing else lately ... beyond heartache."

"And what end to?"

"As you so pointedly observed, a farmer Naoki is not."

"And?"

"Time to learn it is. Here, today, nothing but ashes my mouth within. Something to live for I need to find.

Ca Ira, Haiti

Mardi, 7 June, 2011

Naoki had found a ride from Port au Prince to Léogâne in a flat-bed truck owned by Habitat for Humanity, which was piled high with construction materials. The driver, a volunteer from Georgia, managed to glean a little from Naoki's halting English. When he said "Ca Ira?" the driver nodded and replied. "Near 'nuff. Ah'm set for Léogâne. Y'all can walk the rest of the way. Jest a short piece."

Seeing Naoki's puzzlement, he pointed at himself, then grabbed the steering wheel and said "Léogâne." Then, pointing at his passenger, "You," and walked two fingers across the dusty dashboard, "walk to Ca Ira." He had nodded, encouragingly.

Naoki then smiled and nodded in return.

The road out of Léogâne was familiar from the images he'd seen on GoogleEarth, and though the late afternoon heat was oppressive, he hurried the few kilometers toward his destination. He was more than glad he'd thought to purchase a wide brimmed straw hat from a vendor in Port au, and that he'd dressed for hot weather.

As he neared the village he'd begun to scan side roads for hints that they led toward the farm school, but gradually relaxed and focussed instead on Annejoule. He could feel her presence off toward the south, and sensed that she was conversing with dolphins. Abruptly he knew that the rutted track just past a white-washed cottage was the right one, and he'd soon found himself walking away from the settlement, through scrub and overhanging palms.

A lushly planted field opened on his left and he felt immediate recognition. He stopped and gazed across the neat rows, the blooming tomatoes and beans, the seven-fingered leaf clusters of manioc rising almost to his own height, and the chayote loaded down with small squash.

But there was no sign of the students. He closed his eyes for a few moments. Silver Singer's voice came through.

Annejoule, Annejoule, we sing your name.

Naoki, Naoki, Naoki is near.

I once had a girl, or should I say, she once had me.

She showed me her room, isn't it good Norwegian wood?

Again relying on remembered images from GoogleEarth, he continued along the road, past a small house that he recognized as Dan-Dan's home. Thence to the ford at the muddy stream that is La Rouyonne. Removing his shoes and socks, he stepped into the murky water and enjoyed the feeling as soft mud came up between his toes.

On the far shore he turned right and followed a well-worn path toward the sea.

Annejoule trusted Silver Singer's impression that Naoki was near, but wasn't entirely sure what to make of it. Could it be that her Japanese benefactor was actually here, in Ca Ira? It would be miraculous for someone half a world away to travel to this tiny place.

And yet, she'd felt his grief so powerfully in recent weeks, as if he had never stopped crying since Chicako's death. And she so longed to comfort him, to wrap him in her love. Was Silver Singer merely echoing her own longing?

She and the other students had weeded and wormed and mounded compost long into the afternoon, and then come down to the sea to swim and cool off. The pod of spinners had come to greet them and were frolicking in the surf. Sunset was approaching, and clouds in the east had begun to pick up gold and rose highlights amidst the swirling haze.

We spin, we sing, we laugh.
Sweet dreams are made of these,
Who am I to disagree?
Squiddidle, squidapple, squideemish.
We sing.

Then she saw him. A thin figure in straw hat, white shirt and shorts, carrying a backpack and his shoes as he strode down the shore. He arrived at the rock where the women had laid their clothes, dropped his pack and quickly shed his own clothing.

All the students stared at the naked stranger, skin the color of beach sand, as pale as a clouded moon, walking into the waves. Their modesty was only barely preserved with just their heads above the water. Saraphina guessed aloud. "Annejoule's anmore?"

As Naoki advanced into the water, Annejoule walked toward him, locking eyes, wide with complete amazement. They met, waist deep, and reached toward each other without breaking their gaze, thoughts racing between them. Their hands met, palm to palm.

> *You're here.*
> *Here I am.*
> *So far.*
> *Necessary it was.*
> *Your sadness.*
> *And yours.*
> *Hunger for joy.*
> *Hunger to comfort.*
> *So much you've done here.*
> *So much you've lost.*
> *To you I have come to learn.*
> *We will learn together.*

In the midst of sentences and paragraphs, with mental pictures flashing back and forth between them, their fingers entwined.

Dolphin song coursed through their heads as they touched, both knowing they were both hearing the same sounds.

> *Shimmer and shimmer, spin and spin.*
> *Song of my singing, song of my mother,*
> *Song of begining, song of begetting,*
> *True to be true to be true to be true,*
> *We sing, we sing, we sing the day.*

Wisdom is, wisdom does, wisdom comes,
Fish, fish, fish, fish, fish, fish.

Naoki flattened his hands once more, so they were touching palm to palm, as one of Chicako's haikus welled up within.

Light to dark
Moon pale between drifting clouds
A lover's gentle caress.

A lover?
I don't know.
Closer to me than air, you are.
Or water. You are here.
Heisenberg?
You heard me?
Often. Before ...
Oh. Oh. Before.
I didn't understand and then I did.
When I was ...
Yes and I was in you then, with you, was you, felt you ...
All of the loss. All of the joy.
Your thoughts are my thoughts.
Your mind is my mind.
Light or dark thoughts
Part of one becoming
What then of self remains?

They broke from their protracted gaze, their attention drawn to three dolphins simultaneously leaping high above the waves, twirling as they crashed back into the water. Naoki locked eyese with her again and spoke aloud for the first time, a sentence he had practiced for the duration of his flights around the globe, his attempt to speak in Haitian Creole..

"Chapo'm tonbe nan la me. Rele m Naoki." The simple statement, muddled as it sounded through his Japanese accent, was perfectly clear in her thoughts. *Help me find freedom. Call me Naoki.*

Smiling, she sang the chorus of her mother's song, and then replied in the affirmative. "Libete nou pral jwenn ansanm, Naokisan. renmen lavi m." And then, unbidden and unpracticed, aloud, in fluent Japanese, "Myself Annejoule you call."

About the author

When Cecil Bothwell was elected to Asheville's City Council in 2009 a Confederate, Christian activist attempted to block his induction to office, based on an archaic provision of the North Carolina Constitution which bars from office anyone who "shall deny the being of Almighty God." The trigger was Bothwell's statement concerning personal belief in his critical biography, *The Prince of War: Billy Graham's Crusade for a Wholly Christian Empire* (Brave Ulysses Books, 2007).

The story went viral, reported and repeated around the globe in eight languages, on television, radio and in print. The debate concerning church/state separation erupted in blogs and letters-to-the-editor pages, and hundreds of supporters flooded the author with snail-mail, e-mails and donations to his campaign fund.

In order to address those issues, he next wrote *Whale Falls: An exploration of belief and its consequences* (Brave Ulysses Books, 2010).

Bothwell is an investigative reporter and biographer based in Asheville, and has received national awards from the Association of Alternative Newsweeklies and the Society of Professional Journalists for investigative reporting, criticism and humorous commentary. Former news editor of *Asheville City Paper*, former managing editor of Asheville's *Mountain Xpress* and founding editor of the Warren Wilson College environmental journal *Heartstone*, he served for several years as a member of the national editorial board of the Association of Alternative Newsweeklies and currently serves on the boards of two international educational nonprofit organizations working in Latin America. His weekly radio and print journal, *Duck Soup: Essays on the Submerging Culture*, remained in syndication for 10 years.

He blogs at: bothwellsblog.wordpress .com

Made in the USA
Middletown, DE
15 August 2020